The Keystone

Paul Ntjortjis

ISBN-10: 1519411669
ISBN-13: 978-1519411662

Second Edition – January 2016

Cover design by Paul Ntjortjis & Lorraine Chapman

On their modest thirty-eight foot sailing boat, Callum Williams and his wife Chloe are sailing around the world. While sailing along the coast of Spain, they take on as crew a beautiful young Australian girl who leaves them in mysterious circumstances off the coast of Morocco. This sends them on a journey across the Mediterranean in search of the truth behind her disappearance.

As they travel from Spain to Africa and then to Italy and finally to Greece they attempt to unravel the mystery. Along the way, they become embroiled in a three thousand year old battle between good and evil.

DEDICATION

Dedicated with respect and admiration to all the yachties we have met on our four-year sailing trip to and around the Mediterranean. The 'live aboard' lifestyle, our own experiences, and some of the many people we have met along the way have been the inspiration for this book.

FOREWORD

We have visited all but one of the places in which this story is based on our own sailing yacht and the descriptions are for the most part accurate. Any deviation from fact to fiction is either for dramatic emphasis or due to my misunderstanding.

If you want to checkout our travels and some of the scenes in this novel, visit our blog at:

http://www.sailblogs.com/member/freyaofwight/

Please feel free to leave us a comment, we read them all.

Paul Ntjortjis

ACKNOWLEDGEMENTS

Special mention of course goes to my wife, Lorraine, without whose support and encouragement this book would never have been good enough to publish, but it probably would have been easier to write.

I would also like to thank the experts at Wikipedia and other online sources who provided much of the background information on Ancient Greek legends and a few other details.

CONTENTS

1 - CARTAGENA, SPAIN

Moving at over twenty five knots the Guardia Costiera boat rapidly approaches the sailing yacht Madeline. Her modest thirty eight foot length is dwarfed by the seventy two foot bulk of the powerful Spanish coastguard vessel. The skipper, Callum Williams, calls for his wife Chloe and they furl the foresail and slow down for the coastguard to approach.

"I'm glad it's your day to be skipper," she quips. "You will have to go through the paperwork and answer all their questions."

Callum resists the urge to reply as the white and orange coastguard boat finally slows and comes alongside the Madeline.

There is a considerable swell running and the choppy seas make it difficult for the two boats to get very close. Both boats put fenders out and the coastguard eventually manages to come alongside the Madeline without incident. They throw over a couple of mooring lines to Callum and Chloe who secure them to their boat. With both engines at idle, they can just about hear the coastguard over the noise of the wind and the sea.

"Do you speak English?" one of the coastguards on the boat shouts. Callum responds positively pointing to the red ensign with the Union Jack in the top corner flying on a flagpole on the stern of the boat.

"What is your intended destination?" the coastguard shouts.

"Cartagena," replies Callum.

"Make sure you stay at least five miles offshore until you clear Cabo Tinoso, unless you would like to be shot," he says with a wry smile. Seeing the look of incredulity on their faces, he continues to say. "We are conducting military exercises in the area today and it's for your own safety."

Callum doesn't appreciate the coastguards attempt at humour; he is focused on trying to stop the Madeline being damaged against the coastguard boat as they move in the swell. He decides it would be prudent to laugh at the joke and assures the guard that they will do as he asks. The coastguard moves away but remains close by until it's clear that the Madeline is moving to keep the required distance from shore.

As Chloe steers the boat away from shore Callum goes down below to plot the new course. He briefly glances at the paper charts they keep onboard, but like most sailors of his generation, he enters the new course on the Madeline's electronic chartplotter, which updates automatically with the boats actual (GPS) position in real time. Having entered their original course earlier that morning he is not surprised to see that there isn't a military exercise zone marked on the navigation charts, as there would normally be. Regardless he decides to take the coastguards advice anyway.

The Madeline is a relatively small cruising yacht. Built in the mid 1990s, like most boats of that era she is a strong vessel ideally suited for the round the world trip the Williamses began a few years ago. But being a heavy sailing boat, she only averages around five knots, or about five and a half (statute) miles an hour so the extra distance will add around four to five hours to their journey. Callum hopes that the weather will hold that long but it looks unlikely as the skies are dark and the seas and winds are already beginning to build.

A few hours later Callum's fears have come true, the winds have increased to near storm force and the seas are very rough. They have reefed both sails[1]. With the strong winds and the big waves, some nearly five metres between crest and trough repeatedly hitting the port side, they are struggling to steer the boat.

---

1. Reefing - Temporarily reduce sail size to compensate for high winds.

The Madeline is heeled over[2] with the top sides of the deck on the water line. The waves are breaking over the boat and even though Callum and Chloe are wearing their 'oilies'[3] they are very wet and cold.

Because of the extreme conditions, they are also wearing life jackets and harnesses that are clipped onto strong points in the cockpit to prevent a breaking wave throwing them into the sea.

All of a sudden, a fifty knot gust of wind hits the boat. It overwhelms the rudder and the boat broaches[4]. A big wave hits the side of boat and the Madeline heels over even further, pushing the mast down so that it is nearly horizontal, only just avoiding going into the water. Callum and Chloe are holding on for dear life to avoid being thrown out of the cockpit.

Chloe, as the more natural sailor and better helmsman of the two is on the wheel and as the boat rights itself, and the water drains out of the flooded cockpit, she shouts over the roar of the wind and the sea.

"We can't continue on this course, we need to be running with the wind. If we make straight for Cartagena rather than follow this diversion, the wind would be behind us and we would be taking these waves on the bow. It would be much safer."

2. Heeling - The way a sailboat leans to one side when sailing into the wind
3. Ollies (aka Oilskins) - Waterproof Sailing Suits
4. Broaches - When a boat goes off course and heads into the wind.

Callum readily agrees, "I think I'd prefer to dodge some bullets rather than fight through these waves for any longer," he shouts as another large wave breaks over the side of the boat flooding the cockpit again and getting them even wetter.

Chloe alters their heading towards Cartagena as Callum trims the sails for the new course. This new course cuts straight through the exclusion zone set by the Guardia Costiera. The journey is still very uncomfortable but at least the Madeline is no longer in danger of being overturned and they are now making safe progress towards shore.

****

A few hours later, while the seas are still rough, the wind has eased, the rain has stopped, and visibility has improved. Callum and Chloe are able to take more notice of their passage rather than constantly battling to keep the boat and themselves safe. A mile or so away they can see a couple of other boats. Callum grabs the binoculars and although he has trouble making out the details, it seems that despite the atrocious weather conditions the boats have divers down and are trying to recover something from the sea bed.

"There are two boats out there, a large black motor cruiser and what I think is a dive boat. Whatever it is they are after it must very important, to be diving in these conditions," he says.

They make landfall just after sunset. They have a little difficulty in spotting the red and green lights that mark the entrance channel into the marina against the city lights, but with the aid of the chartplotter they manage to locate the entrance. As they head into the channel, the still heavy seas are making the entrance difficult. Chloe is working hard to keep the boat in the centre of the channel and away from the harbour walls, but they get through safely with no dramas. Thankfully, the marina is well sheltered and once inside the water is much flatter. Even at this late hour, the marina staff are still on duty. They quickly allocate them a berth and because the relatively high winds are making the boat difficult to steer, they help them with the mooring by using their dinghy to push the front of the Madeline round into the berth, stopping their bow from hitting the neighbouring boats. After a quick celebratory bottle of beer and a shower, Callum and Chloe collapse exhausted into bed.

****

They are woken early next morning by the Guardia Civil (customs) who want to register their arrival into the port and to inspect the boat. Three men come aboard rather than the usual one or two. They are very polite but very officious with it and unusually exhibit no signs of having a sense of humour.

They turn to Callum and start asking him some questions. He points to Chloe and says, "She is the captain, not me."

The Guardia officer looks confused, his surprise at a woman being in charge written all over his face. He tries again. "I need to see the papers of the boat and ask you about your previous port," he asks Callum in very passable English.

Chloe steps in with the boat's papers and hands them to the customs officer. He finally gets the point and continues the discussion with her.

Used to the Spanish predilection for form filling she resigns herself to answering the usual questions; Skippers Name: Chloe Williams, Crew List: Callum Williams, Name of Boat: The Madeline, Type of Boat: Sail (Bermudan Sloop), Make & Model: Westerly Ocean Ranger, Number of Masts: 1, Length 11.4m, Beam: 3.7m, Draft: 1.8m, Colour of Hull: White, Number of Berths: 6, Country of Origin: United Kingdom, Number of people on board: 2, Previous Port: Marazon and so on.

The Guardia also ask to inspect their passports and the ship's papers wanting to check its registration document, insurance, VAT status and other documentation. It takes them between twenty to thirty minutes to complete the paperwork. Usually, once the forms have been completed the Guardia move on but not this time. As one of the Guardia asks to check the expiry dates on the ships safety equipment, fire extinguishers, life raft, EPIRB, flares, like jackets and the like, the third man who had remained silent until now starts asking about their journey into Cartagena.

In rapid succession, he barks out a series of questions. "Were you aware of the exclusion zone and did you comply? Did you see anything out of the ordinary?"

"Yes. Of course and no," replies Chloe.

The man turns to Callum, "And what about you? Did you see anything that your wife may have missed?"

Callum having been married for many years, of course doesn't contradict his wife.

Apparently satisfied the Guardia finally leave. Chloe remarks that she thought that they had left all that tedious admin behind when they left their jobs in the UK. "Why we have to go through that every time we arrive in a new port is a mystery to me."

Callum agrees. "Yes and as usual they always seem surprised that a woman might be in charge. Chauvinism is alive and well in sailing and in Spain."

"It's just like when we are coming in to moor. Even though I'm at the helm and obviously in charge of the boat, the marineros (the people providing mooring assistance) will still ignore me and talk to you. I'm not sure if it's annoying or amusing, but it is frustrating."

Callum goes back to talking about the Guardia's visit. "They seemed to be particularly harsh with their questioning and inspections today. All that checking of serial numbers and dates, we've never had that before. It's almost as if they were deliberately trying to put us on edge. I also think it was a bit strange that they were so interested in what we may have seen last night; I wonder what was going on."

"Why don't you check the charts and see if they give you any clues," suggests Chloe.

Callum moves to the chart table and pulling out the paper chart of the area examines it closely. "There are a couple of submarine cables and a deep wreck in the general area. I suspect they were repairing or inspecting the cables," he says.

"Maybe, but if that's all they were doing why were they interested in what we might have seen last night. Either you're being paranoid or there was treasure on that wreck. My money is on the former. Come on, let's go, and explore the town," Chloe says as she starts locking up the boat.

****

Callum and Chloe have just finished lunch in the cockpit of the boat and are pondering a pile of leaflets they collected from tourist information earlier that morning, at least Chloe is. Callum is lying back in the cockpit day dreaming and admiring his wife.

They have been living aboard the Madeline for a few years now and apart from a couple of months either side of Christmas, the weather has been warm enough for them to live outside all of the time. When not actually sailing or maintaining the boat, they spend most of their days, exploring, or lazing about on deck enjoying the sun, just as Callum is doing today.

"We've been together fifteen years," he thinks, "and she is more beautiful then ever." His eyes scan her from top to toe lingering on her short blond hair, radiant blue eyes, and shapely waist. Today she is wearing white knee length shorts and a pretty pink vest that shows her figure off to its best. They make a good couple. Callum is one inch taller than her five foot eight inches and like her, he is in good shape with a honed, but not overdeveloped physique and an almost flat stomach. "I've still got all my own teeth and hair, even if it is going grey," he says to himself.

Their new lifestyle has been good to them both. Apart from the suntans and the obvious lack of stress from no longer working nine-to-five, or more usually much longer, they are both a lot fitter and trimmer than they were. Partly it's the Mediterranean diet, but mostly it's the outdoor lifestyle and not having a car. They walk, cycle, or use public transport to get about. After their first year of cruising, they bought a pedometer to see how far they walked in a typical day ashore. Just doing normal day-to-day tasks such as walking up to the showers and toilets, the supermarket, and laundry they regularly clock up three or four thousand steps. When out exploring or sightseeing, they easily cover around ten miles in about twenty thousand steps. They are both a stone or so lighter and much fitter than when they lived in England.

Callum's thoughts are interrupted by a call from the

pontoon. An olive skinned, brown eyed, dark haired young woman dressed in a similar manner to Chloe but wearing shorter denim shorts and a T-Shirt emblazoned with the logo, 'Life is Precious - Go Live It', approaches the boat. She has noticed that Chloe is reading a leaflet on the Roman ruins of Cartagena.

"G'day," she says from quay. "You mustn't miss the theatre if you are interested in Roman and Punic archaeology and tonight's Semana Santa parades are not to be missed."

"Semana what?" they both respond.

"Literally Holy Week but think Easter parades," she says.

After a few minutes of conversation, they invite her onboard for a coffee. Some hours later, they have moved on from coffee to something stronger. The Williamses are drinking wine, but the girl, Adriane, opted for a beer when she saw the carton of cheap table wine Callum got out of the fridge. They are having a great time with the girl. She is a twenty three year old graduate student from Perth of Greek descent who is taking a few years off to travel before returning to Australia to start work and join the rat race. She has been in Europe for a little while now and is keen to see a slightly rawer side of the Mediterranean. She is full of excitement and anticipation for the colours, smells, and vibrancy of North Africa just a few hundred miles away across the sea. Callum and Chloe tell her a little of their background.

Callum who has just turned forty five is a PHD in engineering and after ten years in industrial manufacturing started work for a global merchant bank advising the banks clients on technology company takeovers and investments. He met Chloe, who is exactly one month younger than he is, at the bank in London where they both worked. She briefly worked there as head of Corporate Social Responsibility. Her role was to ensure that the bank's investments and processes were ethical and supported its employees and the environment. She left after only six months when it became clear that she had no real influence and the role was essentially a public relations one. She has spent most of the last five years championing the rights of the under privileged, supporting charities at home and across the third world. Her ethos was to equip communities and people with the ability to help themselves and never to simply provide handouts. Following the banking crisis of 2008, Callum became increasingly disillusioned with his work and together with Chloe planned his exit from the rat race.

"So how did you get from the bank to here?" asks Adriane.

Chloe responds. "We were spending a long weekend in South Wales and the hotel receptionist told us of a local couple who had spent the last sixteen years sailing around the world. They had just returned to Cardiff Bay marina, which was just along from the hotel. The local TV crews were going to be there and they were having a bit of a party, an open boat, rather than an open house affair. So we went along, got a chance to talk to Clive and Jane and were both hooked by their adventures."

Callum continues the story. "We decided that night that we were going to sail around the world. We set off from England four years ago and have only just made it to Spain. We tend to travel very slowly as we like to explore every place we stop, and Chloe here has to check out all the views," he says with a wink at his wife.

Chloe interrupts, "And you have to spend hours at every archaeological site and museum we come across."

They both laugh it's obviously a long-standing joke between them.

Adriane asks if she could look around the Madeline and they are only too pleased to oblige. Callum and Chloe are very proud of their floating home and while she isn't as glamorous as some more modern and expensive boats, she is solidly built and in good condition for her age. She is well designed both for sailing short handed and for living on.

"We spent about a year looking for the right boat," says Callum. "We saw some boats that had bigger living accommodation, but no storage space. Some were light and fast, but would have been harder for just two people to sail. Other boats perhaps were not as solidly built as the Madeline and so wouldn't take rough seas as well."

"Absolutely, everything in sailing is a compromise, but the Madeline suits as very well," says Chloe.

The Madeline is built of fibreglass with a white hull, teak decks, and a single mast. The cockpit, which is where they are currently sitting, is just behind the mast in the centre of the boat. The cockpit is where the boat is steered and controlled from. Very importantly in bad weather, all the sheets, halyards, and winches that manage the sails can be reached without leaving it. The key instruments showing their course, wind speed, direction, and depth are also here, making her very easy for a crew of two to manage. They continue the tour by going below, entering down a steep set of steps at the front of the cockpit to enter the main saloon. The interior is finished in varnished teak and apart from a few scratches and slightly faded upholstery it looks almost brand new.

To port (left) of the steps is the chart table and navigation area where the rest of the boat's instruments, VHF radio, and radar are located. Behind the chart table is a narrow corridor that leads aft (back) to the main sleeping cabin which has an en-suite toilet and shower or 'the heads' when they feel like using the proper nautical term. To the starboard (right) of the steps is the small galley. The main saloon has seating, which can be configured as an additional double bed and a folding table that can seat up to eight people. At the front of the saloon is another toilet and the forward cabin. In all the Madeline can comfortably sleep six people.

The small diesel engine that is only used to manoeuvre in port or when there is no wind is located behind the steps underneath the cockpit.

Over dinner, Adriane continues to speak of her desire to visit Africa and offers to crew for Callum and Chloe if they feel like going anytime soon. Caught up in the moment they say why not and agree to sail to Morocco in a few days, weather permitting. They finish dinner and it's now much cooler. Chloe changes into jeans and a sweatshirt, lending Adriane a spare pair of jeans and a light coat. She is feeling quietly smug that she can still share clothes with a girl twenty odd years her junior. Together they head off into town to watch the Semana Santa parades.

The parades are like nothing they have ever seen before. Dozens of religious fraternities or orders, each with its own marching band, lead a large wooden float topped with sculptures depicting different scenes from the bible relating to the Passion of Christ or the Sorrows of the Virgin Mary. These floats known as pasos are huge and typically need twenty, thirty, or at times up to fifty people to carry them.

Callum and Adriane are caught up in the music and emotion of the event and are really enjoying the evening. Chloe however is feeling a little uncomfortable and she isn't sure why. Is it the capirote that the people from the fraternities are wearing, long robes with pointed hats and masks that remind her of the Klu Klux Klan or is it the tall dark Arabic looking man that seems to be constantly staring at them?

The Williamses return to the Madeline to get some sleep after agreeing with Adriane that they will head to Morocco the day after tomorrow, if the weather forecast still looks favourable.

****

Callum and Chloe are trying to see Cartagena in a day. They learn that it's where Hannibal set off from to cross the Alps with his elephants but of course for Callum it's all about the Roman history, the theatre, coliseum, and forum. Even Chloe is fascinated by the theatre. It was used by successive generations of people for different purposes over its two thousand year history. Just by looking at the excavated walls, you can see how each successive group of inhabitants modified the buildings of their predecessors.

In 1988 during the construction of a regional arts centre, the remains of the theatre were discovered. Now after fifteen years of archaeological excavations and restorations the theatre is fully open to the public. With just a little direction from a guide, even the untrained eye can see the rich history in the ruins. Their guide is about to explain a little more about the history of the theatre, but her mobile rings. She apologises to the group saying that she has to take the call, explaining that it is the police calling about one of her colleagues who has gone missing.

Callum and Chloe take the opportunity to slip away as she hasn't been the most inspiring of people and continue touring the rest of the ruins on their own.

****

The next morning they are joined by Adriane. After stowing her gear in the forward cabin, they proceed to instruct Adriane on the workings of the boat and their expectations of her as crew. They start by explaining a few of the basic safety related things she needs to know.

"You're a bright girl Adriane, so you've probably noticed that this is a sailing boat," jokes Callum. "That means that there are a few key things to remember. First is that the boom above your head, which carries the mainsail moves. If the weather and sea conditions are a bit fickle, it can move from one side of the boat to the other very quickly and without warning. So keep your head down when moving around on deck.

"Secondly, if we are sailing into the wind the boat will 'heel' or lean over on her side with the toe rails, the outer edges of the deck, in the water. Don't worry it can be a bit uncomfortable but is perfectly normal."

Chloe interrupts, "True but it can also be very exciting. Of course, if she leans too far, the mast could go into the water and the boat roll over. But don't worry, the weight of the keel will turn the boat through three hundred and sixty degrees and she will right herself. It will only happen in extreme weather and we avoid anything like that," she says conveniently forgetting their experiences of the other day.

Adriane is completely unfazed by all this and they continue to show her around the boat explaining the basics of rope handling, how to use the winches, autopilot and VHF radio to send a mayday call if there is an emergency.

"OK," says Callum. "We've done the safety stuff, let's fit your lifejacket, and then get going. The rest you can learn over the next few days. By the time we get to Morocco you will definitely know your way around a sailing boat."

Adriane has been casting anxious glances across the marina as they have been doing the last part of the briefing and has been asking a lot of questions as if to delay them. After a one final glance along the quay, she announces that she has no more questions and that she is ready to cast off if they are, suddenly moving with an urgency that's in stark contrast to her relaxed manner of a few moments ago. As they cast off the lines and pull away from the pontoon, Chloe notices the Arab man she saw at last night's parade running down the quay. As he realises that he has missed the boat, the man stops. He is breathing too heavily to shout, but is obviously very angry.

2 - OF GODS AND MEN

The sun is rising over Mount Olympus. Its jagged peak pierces the ring of clouds that shroud its lower slopes and the sun illuminates the massive pure white marble temple that seems to float effortlessly above it.

Cronus, the leader of the Titans is visiting the home of his son Zeus and his siblings. Cronus is in a foul mood. He is both angry and sorrowful. He has lost count of the number of times he has tried to convince his wayward son to change his ways and has no real confidence that this time he will be any more successful.

Cronus finds his son reclining on a large padded chaise being tended to by three beautiful young women who in truth are little more than adolescents. Much to the chagrin of Zeus, Cronus dismisses the girls with a wave of his hand and they quickly leave the temple thankful that they will not be caught in the coming conflict between two of their gods.

Cronus begins this final attempt to influence his son. Silencing Zeus' protests at the treatment of his slaves, he says, "You have great power my son, but with this power comes great responsibility. The human beings below are not your playthings to be used and discarded on a whim. They are individuals that have as much right to life, freedom, and happiness as you and I. Our forebears, your mother Rhea, and I, together with the rest of the Titans have nurtured these people since before they learnt to talk. They have such promise and you know that it is inevitable that they will eventually succeed us as masters of this planet. You should be helping them develop into people worthy of that destiny, not twist and use them as you, your brothers, and your sisters are doing. I despair of having sired any of you."

"Father they are only mere humans. They live such a brief amount of time, what matters it if we hasten them on their way a little sooner," Zeus replies. "Yes we have used them as you say, but you know our race is dying. Even you and I have mated with our own sisters in an attempt to strengthen our progeny, but you know that isn't enough. The children we have sired with the humans offer our race the chance to go on. The demigods are the future of our people."

Cronus is not fooled by his son's justification.

"You and your brothers bed these human women and men to satisfy your carnal lusts, not for the good of the race. You talk of the demigods and heroes you have sired, but do not mention the countless abominations that you have spawned or the hundreds of women who have died in pregnancy and childbirth.

"You all disgust me. First, you fought amongst yourselves killing hundreds of our people squandering our future in your pointless battles with each other. Now all that remains of our race are a few handfuls of individuals. Too late, you have come to realise that our race is on the brink of extinction. So do you work on leaving a legacy that we can be proud of? No, you declare a truce with your siblings and cousins and decide to cruelly use the humans as proxies to fight your battles for you. I tell you now, that despite your mother's and my love for you all, that a single further transgression will mean that all of the remaining twelve Titans and I will work together to stop you. This is your last warning."

Zeus says nothing, knowing that only a change in behaviour will stay his father's hand. After a while, Cronus rises and with a final look towards Zeus sees the intense concentration behind his impassive frown. He hopes that this signifies that his son is considering his words and that the coming conflict between them will be avoided. He recognises this as wishful thinking and leaves for his home on Mount Othrys with a heavy heart.

Zeus remains seated in silence for sometime looking for a solution to his dilemma. He summons a slave with a clap of his hands and orders her to ask his siblings to gather immediately in his chamber.

****

Zeus, Poseidon, Hades, Hera, Demetia, and Hestia,

the six children of Rhea and Cronus have been discussing the ultimatum. Not one of six siblings has any desire to work for anything other than their own hedonistic pleasure. The thought of gaining satisfaction by improving the lot of others simply does not register with them.

"So we are agreed then," concludes Zeus. "Our father is not bluffing this time. The Titans will attempt to kill us all if we do not change and do as they ask. We are not prepared to do so, so we have no choice but to defend ourselves. I see no option but to kill them before they kill us."

The five other Olympians all signal their agreement. The prospect of killing their parents doesn't warrant even a moment's hesitation.

****

So began a ten year battle between the Titans and the Olympians. The war soon drifted into a stalemate, their titanic battles laying waste to a large part of what was later to become known as Thessaly in Greece. The war turned when Zeus managed to free two of Cronus' ancient enemies, Cyclopes and the three Hecatonchires, from their prison within the earth. The Hecatonchires were fifty-headed one hundred-handed giants and like Cyclopes were siblings of Cronus. The Hecatonchires lent their great strength to the fight and Cyclopes forged powerful weapons for Zeus and his brothers. It was these weapons that enabled the Olympian's final triumph. For Zeus he fashioned a special thunderbolt that could throw bolts of lightening with great force. For Poseidon, he created a trident, or three-pronged spear, which could defeat any enemy and for Hades a magic helmet that could make him invisible.

These weapons turned the war to the Olympian's favour and eventually the Titans were defeated. Cronus surrendered on condition that Zeus spared the lives of the surviving Titans and he agreed, initially imprisoning them in Tartarus guarded by the Hecatonchires and Cyclopes. However, Zeus had no plans to risk their escape and once they were all in the same place and without a second thought he and Poseidon destroyed them all using the Trident and the Thunderbolt.

Following their final victory, the three brothers divided the world amongst themselves. Zeus ruled the sky and the air and he was recognised by the other two as king of the gods. Poseidon was given the sea and all of the waters, whereas Hades was given the Underworld, the realm of the dead. The earth was common to all of them and became the stage for the sick games they played with human lives.

****

Following the release of his siblings, the Cyclopes and the Hecatonchires, it soon became clear to Cronus that the war would ultimately turn against him. He urged Prometheus and his brother Epimetheus, the two sons of the Titans, Themis, and Iapetus, to switch sides and ally with the Olympians.

Cronus tasked them to protect the human race and to temper the worst excesses of the Olympians. Humanitarian to the core the two brothers agreed and secretly worked to fulfil Cronus' request while outwardly adopting the behaviour of their new allies.

The two brothers recruited and trained a select cadre of humans to help them in their sacred task and to carry on their work through the ages.

3 - MAN OVERBOARD

Once out of sight of land, Adriane is very relaxed and proves to be a good companion and capable crewmember. "How are you feeling Adriane?" asks Callum. "I always take sea sickness pills on long passages would you like one?"

Adriane laughs, "I'm fine thanks, but I'm confused. You live on a boat with no plans to return to normal life for years and you get seasick. Are you sure you've chosen the right lifestyle?"

"Absolutely," both Callum and Chloe reply together, "Beats working any day."

It's around two hundred and fifty nautical miles from Cartagena to Smir, in Morocco, where they plan to make landfall, and the journey is expected to take around fifty hours. There is little wind and while they currently have both of the sails out, it looks as if the engine will be on for the whole trip. Chloe, whose turn it is to be skipper today, sets up a three hour watch system. She chooses to have two people on watch with one person asleep or relaxing for three hours before it's the next persons turn. By nightfall, the wind has died completely and they are motoring with only the mainsail raised. It's not giving them any assistance but it will make it easier for other boats to see them. It's completely dark with the boat's navigation and instrument lights being the only artificial lights they can see.

It's just after midnight and Adriane and Chloe are in the cockpit on watch while Callum is asleep. The autopilot is doing the steering and there is very little to do apart from keep a lookout, admire the stars and chat. Adriane is entranced by the experience, especially by how the moonlight dances in the wake of the boat behind them. She is lying on her back staring at the stars. She raises her hand and points.

"Look Chloe, there's the constellation of Andromeda and over there Argo and there Taurus the bull."

Chloe is impressed. Like all good sailors she can find the Big Dipper and by following the 'pointer stars' on its end, can find the Pole Star and hence can sail north without the compass, but that's her limit.

Adriane continues to tell her the stories behind the constellations. "Andromeda," she says, "Was an Ethiopian princess the daughter of Cassiopeia. Her mother offended the gods by boasting that her daughter was more beautiful than the Nereids. So Poseidon chained Andromeda to some rocks and sent a sea monster to eat her. Perseus saw her there, instantly fell in love, slew the beast, and carried her off and then married her. The gods, as a memorial to this brave act, set the whole family amongst the stars as constellations."

Chloe asks where she got this encyclopaedic knowledge of the ancient Greeks from. "It's a bit of a family obsession," she replies with a grin.

Adriane asks Chloe about their life before sailing. Chloe skirts over the time she spent working for the bank and at other companies.

"I mostly enjoyed it at the time, but I got much more satisfaction helping out in my local community and doing voluntary work with the few charities I actively supported. Its quite funny really, a friend asked me to help out with some admin for a local charity that worked on rural development projects in Africa. I was happy to give a few hours of effort but I soon felt like a fish on a line. Once they got their hook into me, they started reeling me in. I was asked to do more and more.

"Soon I was one of the trustees. I was so inspired by the difference this small charity made to people's lives that I felt less and less engaged at work. Callum was very supportive and said that I should follow my heart and leave regular full time employment if that's what I really wanted." She says.

"So you did the charity work and Callum supported you both then?" asks Adriane.

"Absolutely not! I love Callum, but I could never give

up my independence. I did short term contracts, usually six months on, six months off so I'd have the time to give. After a while I was offered a few part time paid positions with some NGOs working in Africa that meant I could cut down on the contracting."

"That so cool, it must have been very fulfilling," says Adriane with more than a hint of envy in her voice. "So why did you give it up and go sailing it must have been very hard?"

Chloe is now in full flow. "It was and it wasn't. We did make a difference, but it was still so much less than what is really needed. The NGOs and charities are so tied up in red tape. They constantly have to raise money and then account for how it's being used. Balancing the conflicting priorities, fighting entrenched political systems that seemed to work against rather than for their people, it was all so exhausting and emotionally draining, I needed a break.

"I'm not sure what our long-term plan is but in a few years we both intend to go back and do something along those lines together. Perhaps set up our own project on the ground, especially if we can find a way to make it self funding. The communities can then decide how to invest the profits without it getting diluted by the administrative and political problems faced by the big charities."

Adriane is impressed. "Wow, that's amazing. I'm sure you will think of something and be successful. I wish I could do something similar but can't see myself being able to give something back for a little while yet. I have a job to finish and a lot of family commitments that I can't ignore. So what's Callum's story?" she asks before Chloe can quiz her about her commitments.

"I'm sure he will tell you himself over the next few days," responds Chloe. "But now your watch is over and you should go down below and get some sleep. Make sure you wake Callum as you go down."

Adriane wakes Callum who replaces her on watch. As he settles into the cockpit with his wife, she remarks that Adriane is a natural sailor and very knowledgeable for such a young and beautiful girl. "It's not fair," she says.

Callum smiles and tells his wife to stop fishing. "You're more beautiful, intelligent, and caring then any woman I've met. She is almost twenty years younger than you though, perhaps I should think about trading you in for a younger model."

Chloe throws her sailing gloves at Callum who ducks just in time.

The following day the Madeline is making good progress and should make landfall in Smir just after dawn. Adriane suggests that she would be happy to take the night watch on her own if they both want to catch up on their sleep. As it's so calm and she seems to be a natural, Callum and Chloe readily agree. Callum asks her to wake them before they get within ten miles of land.

Adriane starts her solo night watch and as Chloe is getting into bed, she sees Adriane talking into her phone. Just as she is drifting to sleep she realises there shouldn't be a mobile phone signal this far out to sea. What is a twenty three year old backpacker from an apparently modest background doing with a satellite phone?

A little while later, Adriane checks that Callum and Chloe are fast asleep and quietly lowers the dinghy off its davits on the back of the boat. After a final check that all is well with the Madeline and that she is on course, Adriane climbs aboard the dinghy and casts it adrift taking only the clothes she is wearing, her satellite phone, and a small bag. The Madeline motors on under autopilot.

After an hour or so Callum wakes and goes up on deck to check on how things are going. He soon realises that Adriane is no longer on board and wakes Chloe.

"Man overboard!" he shouts and grabs their large one million candlepower torch. In what he knows will be a hopeless attempt to spot Adriane in the water, he scans the light around the boat and notices that the dinghy is missing just as Chloe shouts up to him from the navigation table where she was about to make a mayday call on the VHF radio.

"The dinghy is missing," says Callum.

"There is a note from Adriane here," responds Chloe.

Chloe opens the note and a number of banknotes drop to the floor. She ignores the money and reads the note out aloud. "I'm sorry for leaving this way, but please don't worry about me, I will be all right. Thank you both for bringing me this far and for your excellent company and hospitality. I've left you one thousand Euros to cover the cost of the dinghy. For all our sakes, please don't tell anyone that I crossed this far with you. Your friend and shipmate, Adriane."

"What do we do now?" asks Chloe.

"First we see to the boat and make sure we are on course and that there are no immediate dangers about, then I think we check her things," Callum replies.

They are still ten miles from the coast of Morocco and there are no other vessels around so Callum joins Chloe down below who has retrieved Adriane's backpack and emptied its contents over the bunk.

All Callum can see on the bunk is a small toilet bag, a t-shirt, a change of underwear, a load of books, and some nautical charts.

"It doesn't look as if she ever intended to spend more than a day or two with us," he says. "And it's obvious where her knowledge of the ancient Greeks and Romans comes from. These are all serious reference books. Some are quite specialist and I'm surprised to see them outside of a university library."

On examining the charts he sees that a lot of ancient shipwreck sites have been highlighted, some have names against them, Fernando Castertano and Asterion being the most common.

Its clear to Callum and Chloe that Adriane had planned to jump ship all along and so probably isn't in any danger. If they report the incident to the Moroccan or Spanish authorities they could be in big trouble, after all they don't really know anything about her apart from what she has told them. She could be anything from a drug runner, to a spoilt heiress or a foolish young adventurer. There is nothing in the records at Cartagena to suggest they had another crewmember on board so with a lot of misgivings they decide to do as Adriane asks and not report the incident. They continue on to Smir.

4 - SAILING INTO THE SUNSET
(5 Years Earlier)

It's nearly nine pm and Callum has just returned home after yet another very long day at work. He left home at five thirty this morning to catch the six fifteen train into London for the first of many meetings. He is exhausted. Not only has this hectic schedule become the norm over the last few months, he can't see any sign of it easing. He is currently advising two of the bank's clients on three potential takeover targets and there are more on the horizon.

Chloe gives him a welcome home kiss and offers him a glass of wine, a Chablis Premier Cru. She says nothing for a few minutes giving her husband time to unwind a little from of the rigours of his day. Her day has also been stressful and emotionally draining; she has been fighting red tape all day at the charity but knows that if she doesn't give Callum some time he won't 'hear' what she has to say.

"Well that was another pointless day," he says, settling into a rant that Chloe knows will be very similar to the others she has heard a number of times over the last year. "The day started with a 'peer review' meeting. I had to explain the technical merits and weaknesses of Harptree Electronic Control Systems, one of the current takeover targets, to a bunch of people who had no interest in what I was saying. The bank's processes require that my recommendations are peer reviewed. But no one else in the team is an electronics or manufacturing specialist, so none of them have the background to intelligently comment. If I'm being generous, maybe they could have spotted a hole in my investigations and analysis, if they tried, but not one of them paid any real attention to my presentation. They spent the whole meeting playing with their phones, answering email and taking calls without even an apology. It's always the same. Unless something directly affects their career or bonus, they don't even pretend interest.

"Then I had to attend a health and safety training session on the new office chairs and how to adjust and sit on them. I felt so sorry for the guy from the facilities team. He got nothing but sarcastic comments from everybody. He then made the mistake of asking if anybody had any other health and safety queries and he just got another thirty minutes of abuse over why we can't have a toaster or a kettle in the kitchens. It's just so petty. The rest of the day was pretty much like that as well. You know the really sad thing, I think the lesson on how to sit at a desk, was the most valuable thing I did all day. To cap it all the trains were delayed and it took hours to get home. I've just about had enough. At least we are going to Wales tomorrow for our long weekend away. Please cheer me up and tell me about your day, I need to hear that at least one of us has done something useful today."

Chloe has heard similar speeches from Callum before. It seems to her that at least half of his working day is spent in unproductive activities, half of the remainder in travelling to and from the office or client sites and only a few hours a day actually doing what he is paid to do. She isn't surprised he is frustrated.

"I'm sorry, I'd love to have some good news, but we still haven't got the funding for our new project in Mozambique. All we got back was yet another questionnaire and a set of instructions from the trust fund. They want us to adjust our audit process and controls. The trouble is each of the funds has their own way of doing things, so we need to have separate processes for each of our funding streams. The overhead is crippling us and we are going to have to find another part time administrator. Each new project we get started means that I spend more and more time on admin and less on the front line. I know the trusts have to perform due diligence on us to ensure their money is being put to good use, I wouldn't expect anything less, but meanwhile people are going hungry and getting sick. All this form filling and bureaucracy is driving me mad. I need this weekend away as much as you," she says.

"Perhaps what we need is a much longer break. So much of what we do seems to be totally unproductive," says Callum. "At least what you're doing is ultimately worthwhile, but what am I doing? Working all the hours god sends and for what? I don't get to see enough of you or this lovely house that we spent years looking for. We see them so rarely, I can hardly remember what most of our friends or family look like. What do we get from living like this? A couple of nice cars, some Swiss watches and a fantastic view from the balcony that we've barely seen all winter because it's dark when we leave home and dark when we get back."

Chloe agrees with Callum and they decide to talk about it some more over their weekend way. Having let off steam, they both relax a little and enjoy the wine and each other's company, before heading off to bed.

****

They start their break in Cardiff and as suggested by their hotel they head to the marina in Cardiff Bay to watch the return of Clive and Jane who have just returned to Wales after sailing around the world.

They have never thought of sailing off into the sunset before, but after talking to Jane, the freedom of the lifestyle grabs them. They decide there and then that it's their escape route from the rat race and it's the life for them.

"It seems perfect to me," says Callum. "We can take our home with us as we travel, no more lugging backpacks or suitcases around. When we are bored with the view, we can just move the boat until we find a new and better one. We should never get bored, as we will always have new places to explore and cultures to experience. I can't wait to explore the Med, all those ancient Roman and Greek sites to see."

"Absolutely, but aren't you forgetting something. We can't sail and haven't got a clue about boats," says Chloe. Before Callum can respond, she continues. "But we've never let little technicalities like that get in our way before. First, we need to book on some sailing courses and get some practical experience. Second, we need to buy a boat and then we are going to have to find a way to pay for all this. We don't want to be working once we set off. Oh. And what are we going to do with the house and all our stuff?"

They talk all through the weekend and spend hours researching things online. By the end of their short break, they have a tentative plan and it all looks possible. They will have to change their lifestyle. Give up the posh cars, clothes and fine dining, but Callum realises that he really only wanted those trappings of success to justify working so hard. For Chloe it's never been about the material things. It will take them a couple of years to get ready to go, but with a goal to aim for, all of a sudden the frustrations of their working lives seem bearable.

****

Acquiring basic sailing skills was easy. The RYA (Royal Yachting Association) has a progressive syllabus of training courses that take people from novice to 'Yacht Master'. After their first couple of practical sailing courses they are both hooked, despite Callum's tendency to seasickness. They quickly complete the first set of courses and within only a few months have qualified as 'Day Skippers'. This qualification has equipped them with the knowledge to skipper a sailing boat for short coastal passages of around a day in length. They now know the basics of boat handling, navigation, tides, international regulations at sea and a little on how to read the weather. What they lack is experience.

They join a local sailing club to get some time on the water, and while they have some fun they soon realise they are not getting the right sort of experience. They have learnt a little more about how to set the sails and to 'read' the wind and waves a little better, but they are not learning enough about boat handling, passage planning or how to maintain a boat.

Understandably, the boat's owners got a little concerned when Callum or Chloe tried to manoeuvre their expensive boats in a tight marina or were helming the boat in difficult conditions. The owners would either take over or tell them exactly what to do in minute detail. There was only one thing for it they had to get a boat of their own.

They bought a cheap, small twenty eight foot boat that they sailed around the UK coast for a season. Once they were sure that this was the life they wanted, they sold this boat and started looking for a bigger boat, eventually buying the Madeline.

It took them a further year to equip the Madeline and

get her ready for their live aboard cruising lifestyle. Knowing that they would need to be pretty much self-sufficient at sea, after all there isn't the equivalent of the AA or any other emergency services in the middle of the ocean; they both learn how to do all the routine boat maintenance. They also take some specialist sea survival and maritime first aid courses and buy a few more advanced books. One of which that they hope never to need, tells them how to perform minor surgery and even amputations at sea!

Just before they are ready to set off, the bank offers Callum a redundancy package which helps ease their finances a little. They sell their dream home and purchase two small properties that they plan to rent out. The income from these properties and their remaining savings, while modest, should fund their adventure for a few years.

Just over two years after deciding to sail off into the sunset together, Callum, Chloe, and the Madeline are ready to go. They have agreed their passage plan for the next few years, it's very simple - 'Head south and keep land to the left'.

They set off from Falmouth to cross the English Channel. Eighteen hours later, they make landfall in L'aberwach in Brittany and their adventure has begun.

5 - NORTH AFRICA

Adriane waits for the Madeline to motor away and once it is a mile or two ahead, she makes a call on her satellite phone and after giving her GPS position lies back to enjoy the wait.

A few hours later, she calls again and gives her latest position. The sun is just on the horizon and Adriane has been savouring the sunrise and the solitude. Callum and Chloe have told her of these magical moments at sea and now she really understands the beauty of the open ocean. She is almost disappointed to see a large white motor boat in the distance. She opens the dry bag and removes one of the two orange smoke flares it contains. She pulls the tag on the flare and is rewarded with a plume of orange smoke drifting into the air. The motor boat adjusts its course and a few minutes later Adriane is helped aboard by a white clad steward.

"Welcome back aboard the Minos ma'am, your father is waiting for you on the skydeck. Breakfast is being prepared and will be ready in thirty minutes," he says as he hands her a tall crystal glass full of champagne and freshly squeezed orange juice.

The Minos is a forty metre Sunseeker motor yacht and is in a completely different league to the Madeline. Costing over twenty million pounds, it's nearly four times longer, three times as wide and is built over three decks. It's the height of luxury with accommodation for ten people in five en-suite staterooms plus accommodation for eight crewmembers.

After freshening up in her luxurious cabin, Adriane dresses herself in a long flowing sundress and joins her father, Professor Theos, on the skydeck. He is a powerful muscular man whose large dark brown eyes sparkle with intelligence and wisdom. While he is obviously pleased to see his daughter, his smile does not dispel the look of weariness and sadness he perpetually carries. Like Adriane, he has a small tattoo of a stylised maze in a triangle on his upper arm. She recounts her last few days with the Williamses and the professor seems quietly pleased.

"Did you leave enough clues?" he asks.

"Yes," she replies, "But they seem like genuinely nice people and it's a shame to drag them into this."

The professor nods but they both agree they had no real choice.

****

The Madeline has arrived in Morocco and has pulled alongside the reception berth at Marina Smir one of the few ports of entry on Morocco's Mediterranean coast. After checking in at the marina, Callum is directed to the immigration office with the ship's documents and their passports.

The office is located in a small concrete building on the quay that is in need of more than a little tender loving care. The paint is peeling off the walls, the windows cracked and the few light bulbs that are working seem to add to, rather than dispel the gloom and decay. The immigration officer is sitting behind a small desk surrounded by a mountain of paper. In the corner sits a fifteen year-old PC that is covered in dust. It's not turned on. A small electric fan spins slowly in a vain attempt to cut through the stifling heat of the room. After first trying in Arabic, the immigration officer greets him very politely in Spanish. He carefully records the same information just collected by the marina office, but this time in triplicate. The carbon sheets he is using to make the copies are very worn and after a while, he discards them and manually completes each sheet in turn. Callum waits patiently, knowing that any sign of impatience or frustration would only lengthen the process. After about forty minutes, the immigration officer finally stamps their passports and directs Callum to the customs office where the whole process is repeated.

Eventually Callum is sent back to the marina office clutching a wad of official forms. A few more stamps on the forms and nearly two hours after arriving at the reception quay, the marina staff are finally able to show them to their allotted visitor berth.

Marina Smir is located in a modern resort complex frequented by wealthy Moroccans and the occasional foreigner. Unlike the official government buildings on the quay, the development is well maintained and welcoming, even if it's not the rawer side of the Mediterranean they were expecting. Callum and Chloe have just finished putting the boat to bed after their two day crossing when a camel walks down the quay. It stops and looks over at them as if to welcome them to Morocco. Its handler is running to catch up and he turns to Callum and offers them a camel ride or a photo opportunity for only twenty Dirham (about two Euros). They decline but are very pleased to meet their new friend.

The Williamses have been approached by a local taxi driver called Mohamed who speaks excellent English, Spanish, and French in addition to his native tongue of Darija Arabic. He is very friendly and a good source of information but they are under no illusion that for him they are the only potential source of income around today. He recommends a visit to the small fishing town of M'diq, which they can get to by bus today, but suggests that tomorrow they should hire him to take them into the mountains to the town of Chefchaouen. It's a beautiful old mountain town, with a large traditional souk, and where every house is painted light blue. Callum is sold on the idea.

"One of the problems with travelling by boat," he says, "is that you only see the edges of a country. It would be good to head inland for a day."

****

Back in Cartagena, a mobile phone rings. An Arabic looking man answers with a terse, "Asterion."

The voice on the phone starts speaking in hushed but urgent tones. "We have found the boat, but the girl is not there, only the two English infidels."

"I don't care for your religious classifications, remember that I too am an infidel, and so just stick to the facts. Where are they?" Asterion barks.

"Smir, in Morocco," the caller replies.

"Do nothing to alert them, but make sure you do not lose them. I will be with you as soon as I can."

They continue talking for some moments more, discussing Asterion's arrival and their next steps.

****

Callum and Chloe walk up the hill out of the complex to the main road where they find the bus stop and only a few minutes later they are in M'diq. There, their first stop is a stroll through the fishing harbour where today's catch is just being unloaded. They spot a crate of bonito being taken into a harbour side cafe. The cafe has a large barbecue on the pavement and soon the smell of cooking fish is irresistible. They grab a table and in their best Spanish order some barbecued fish and bread for lunch. An almost prefect meal for only a couple of euro each, spoilt only by the lack of a glass of wine.

Outside of a few specialist shops and the western tourist resorts, Morocco is a dry country. Luckily, the Madeline is well stocked with wine. Chloe made it clear to Callum right at the start of their relationship that running out of cold white wine was a divorceable offence.

After lunch they wander along the sea front past the recently completed, but yet to open marina and into the narrow winding streets of the old town. As Chloe turns to look at a street stall, she spots Mohamed walking behind, as if he is following them, but he waves and comes over to speak to them.

"I saw you walking in the street," he says with a smile. "Did you notice the new marina? It's been complete for about a year now, but they still haven't opened it to the public. A few government officials and some very wealthy people used it for a few days, but it's been empty ever since. What a waste. I was about to head back to Smir myself and could offer you a lift back at half price."

Callum looks at Chloe who obviously has a lot more exploring to do. "I don't think we are ready to return yet, we'll catch the bus in a few hours or so," he says.

Mohamed bids them a cheery farewell and walks off. "Strange bumping into the only person we know in

Morocco isn't it. Almost as if he was looking out for us," says Callum.

Chloe, who is too wrapped up looking at the embroidered leather Moroccan slippers on the stall to think about Callum's statement, replies by handing Callum a pair of the shoes and asking if they would make a good present for her father. They finish their wandering before the end of the afternoon and return to the boat for a quiet evening of people watching from the quay.

When they arrive back on the Madeline, they find what seems like the whole of the local population, is out for a stroll or promenade along the quay. The Madeline is the star attraction with people standing alongside and taking photos with her in the background. A few braver souls actually attempt to climb onboard, unaware that the owners are down below. They surprise and shoo off most of these unwelcome visitors, but do allow those that knocked first to come aboard and pose for a photo. They are particularly pleased when they see the smile of one five year old boy who they allow to stand behind the wheel as if he is steering. By suppertime, the resort is deserted and they have an early night.

****

The next morning, Mohamed turns up in his ramshackle twenty year old white Mercedes taxi to take them inland into the Rif Mountains and on to Chefchaouen. As they drive along the road pedestrians frequently try to flag them down. It is common practice to share taxis in Morocco if they are going in your general direction, but when you are Western tourists, you get exclusive use of the car. On the way they stop at Al Hamra.

Most days this is a just field by a truck stop on the junction of two roads, but it comes alive every Wednesday for a Berber market. The stalls are full of wonderful food, from vegetables and cuts of meat, to live chickens and goats. Crowds of Berbers gather around the larger livestock, mostly donkeys and horses, making bids in an informal but obviously very serious auction. In addition to food and animals, you can seemingly buy all the other material essentials of life, from second hand clothes, used mobile phones, household goods, and toiletries to furniture. Their favourite was a stall weighed down with a huge pile of unpaired second hand Wellington boots. Callum and Chloe loved every minute of it, despite the fact that it was chaos, they were constantly dodging the mud, and the Berbers dressed in their traditional robes.

"They look like obi-one-kin-obi from Star Wars," thinks Chloe.

An hour or so after leaving the market, they catch their first glimpse of Chefchaouen and immediately fall in love with it. The blue houses cling to the steep mountainsides and seem to be a very natural part of the landscape. Mohamed explains that the houses are painted blue to discourage mosquitoes. Callum and Chloe are not convinced, thinking that the lack of them may have more to do with the altitude rather than the colour of the buildings.

They arrive in Chefchaouen itself just before lunch and head straight for the souk. The sights of the souk captivate them and although they find the leather tannery interesting, the smell was more than a little overpowering. Mohamed has told them of a carpet shop they should visit which has a large roof terrace from which they can see over the rooftops of the city. As they enter the carpet shop they are greeted by a man dressed in traditional costume that is more than happy to take them up to see the view.

On the way down from the roof terrace, he insists that they have a mint tea before they leave and shows them into a large room with piles of carpets. "Here comes the hard sell," Callum says and Chloe smiles in agreement.

The man returns with the mint tea which is ridiculously sweet, but anxious not to insult they drink it and say its lovely. The man shows them a few samples, but obviously, they have no space on the Madeline for a Persian carpet and they get up to leave. The Arab man insists they stay and he will show them some smaller ones. He leaves the room and locks the door behind him.

Callum and Chloe are confused. They try the other doors and windows, which are all locked and far too strong to be forced. Initially they think the shopkeeper doesn't want them sneaking away while he is out of the room, but after a few minutes have passed and he hasn't returned they begin to get angry and then worried.

Their shouts for help can either not be heard over the sounds of the souk or are being ignored. Resigned to the situation they sit down on a pile of the finest carpets and wonder how long it will be before Mohamed starts looking for them.

After some time the sun begins to set and they are now hungry and scared in addition to being angry. As the mosques start the evening call to prayer, the door opens and an Arab man enters the room, flanked by four other men. A picture of a shark and four barely tame gorillas flashes through Chloe's mind. It's the man from the parades and the harbour. One of the gorillas looks familiar, but his keffiyeh (Arab headdress) and the tension makes it difficult for her to place him.

"Let me introduce myself," says the shark in perfect unaccented English. He is over six foot tall and while his skin is a Mediterranean olive colour, his aura is one of intense darkness.

"My name is Asterion. Be under no illusions you are in grave danger. If you wish to return to your boat unharmed you will answer all my questions truthfully, fully and without hesitation."

Callum gets up and walks towards Asterion. "What's the meaning of this? You can't treat us like this. You-"

he starts to say.

One of the gorillas steps towards Callum before he can reach Asterion and cuffs him across the face, the force of the blow sending him falling to the ground. Luckily a pile of carpets breaks his fall and apart from a bright red welt and developing bruise across his face, he is unhurt.

"I hope that you now understand how to behave," says Asterion.

Callum pulls himself up and is about to object again, but Chloe jumps in and says, "Just ask your questions."

Asterion questions Callum and Chloe in great detail for nearly two hours, constantly going over the same ground in an attempt to catch them out. He wants to know about their recent movements especially their entry in to Cartagena and in particular about Adriane. They tell him everything. Initially he suspects they are holding out on him but after a while, he believes they may be telling him the truth. Eventually they are bundled into a brand new black Range Rover and followed by another large four-by-four car and flanked by four police motor cycles they are driven back to Smir and the Madeline.

Asterion demands to see Adriane's belongings, in particular her books and charts. They lay everything out on the dining table in the main saloon. He is very interested in the charts, especially the highlighted references to ancient shipwrecks in the Balearic Islands. Callum and Chloe are frightened but are also intrigued by what is happening. Finally, Asterion seems satisfied and gets up from table. He reaches into his robes and removes a handgun and a silencer. He slowly screws the silencer onto the barrel of the gun and very slowly and deliberately places it on Chloe's forehead.

"Are there any other charts or books?" he asks.

Callum and Chloe are no longer frightened; they are terrified. But strangely the strongest emotion they are feeling is anger. They have never been so helpless before.

"No," they both reply to Asterion's final question. "You have everything."

"I thought as much," Asterion says "I just needed to be sure."

He pulls the trigger of the gun.

****

On the Minos Adriane and her father are having their evening meal, Adriane is telling the professor more about her time with the Williamses and in particular about Chloe's philanthropic work. She is just about to tell her father about how she would like to do something similar when a young female steward enters. The girl is nearly six foot of solid muscle and moves with the control and grace of a ballerina or a gymnast. She waits to be addressed.

"Excuse me professor our agents in Morocco have just informed us that Asterion has made contact with the Williamses."

"If it all it goes to plan, Asterion will be preoccupied for some weeks, hopefully months, and we can work freely for a while. Ellie, please ask the captain to set course for Oristano, best possible speed," he replies.

Leaving his dinner, he moves to the library and removes a large-scale paper chart of the west coast of Sardinia. He has marked a shipwreck by a small island just outside Oristano bay.

"The wreck is spread across a small area of the sea bed, at depths of between fifteen and twenty five metres," he says.

"We will be able to work with normal SCUBA gear and compressed air so the diving will be relatively easy. I'm pretty certain that if the university divers found and retrieved the casket it would have caused a sensation and we would have heard. I'm sure its still there on the seabed somewhere. Soon it will finally be back in our possession after all these years."

For the first time in many years, the worry lines on the professor's face seem to fade a little.

Adriane is standing by the window, staring north in the

direction of Morocco across the sea. Theos notices the look of sadness and concern on her face.

"Don't worry," he says, "When this is over, we will make it up to them."

"If they are still alive," Ariadne thinks to herself.

****

There is a click but no explosion. The gun isn't loaded and Callum and Chloe collapse in a mixture of shock and relief. Asterion considers for a while, packs up all of Adriane's belongings into her backpack, and passes it to one of the gorillas. He turns to the Williamses and fixing them with his dark stare tells them to say nothing to anyone, to leave Smir in the morning and not to return to Spain or visit the Balearic Islands for a few years at least. He walks off the boat without waiting for a response or even a backward glance, so sure is he that his little demonstration has ensured that they will play no further part in what's to come.

The cars and motorbikes drive off and Callum and Chloe are left alone on the Madeline in an uneasy silence. After a few moments, Callum is the first to pull himself together. He walks over to the galley and opens the fridge. He pours two large glasses of white wine. Handing one to Chloe they both drink them down in a few gulps. After topping up the glasses, Callum takes Chloe into his arms. It takes a little while longer before the wine softens the shock of Asterion's theatrics and they start to talk, to try to make sense of the last few days.

"Adriane is no more a backpacker from Perth than you are the pope," Chloe says. "She is obviously mixed up with some seriously nasty people. What do you think this is all about, drugs, illicit treasure, or what?"

"Not drugs," replies Callum. "If this is about drugs, why are they interested in all those shipwrecks? I think they are looking for ancient artefacts, probably for private collectors. I'm sure there are millionaire collectors out there that would pay big money for rare pieces. Or perhaps you're right, there could be treasure on those sunken ships."

"I agree, but would they really kill for it? I was really terrified when he had that gun to my head," says Chloe.

With more certainty in his voice than he is actually feeling Callum replies. "I was too, but now, I don't think for a second he was planning to kill us. He just meant to scare us, which he certainly did. I felt so helpless seeing you in that position. It's been like that all day."

They discuss what to do next. Should they heed Asterion's 'advice', should they head to the Balearic Islands to try to find out what's happening or go to the authorities. They immediately dismiss reporting the incident to the Moroccans fearing that they may not be able to leave the country for months, besides those looked like genuine police motor bikes flanking the cars. Whoever Asterion is, he obviously has some powerful connections. They briefly consider returning to Spain and reporting to the police there, but remembering the incident with the boat in the restricted zone and the over zealous interest of the Guardia Civil - that's where they saw the gorilla before - they decide that discretion is probably their safest option. Besides, they have no proof and if they were believed, they would be in a lot of trouble for not reporting Adriane's passage and disappearance.

So they decide to heed Asterion's advice and leave Morocco. "Well I think Adriane meant Asterion to find her stuff," says Callum. "If it was that important and secret why did she leave it on board? I think we were setup to be a diversion from the moment she saw us in Cartagena. We now know Asterion was watching her during the Semana Santa parades and he was on the quay as we left."

"Yes, that seems obvious now. I think all those detailed questions on the pontoon were delaying us until she was certain that he would see her leave with us. But what are we going do now?" asks Chloe.

"I don't think we should go to the authorities here or in Spain, but we've been kidnapped and threatened at gunpoint. I think we should tell someone, but how do we do that without getting into trouble?" says Callum.

"Why don't we head across back to Gibraltar? It's only thirty miles away and talk to those friends of your Auntie Phyllis, Harry, and Val. As an ex copper she'll know what's best to do."

Callum agrees with his wife and they head to their cabin to try to grab a few hours sleep before sunrise.

6 - ON ROUTE TO MAJORCA

Onboard another luxurious motor yacht, Asterion is sitting across a large oak table from an excited and enthusiastic older man. At around twenty five metres in length, Asterion's Sunseeker Predator motor yacht seems perfectly suited to the man. Its sleek powerful lines and all black colouring make it look very ominous and threatening on the water. It's making its way from Morocco to the Balearic Islands at well below its maximum speed of forty five knots. Despite carrying over thirteen hundred gallons of diesel fuel, they can't make the journey without stopping for more. At its recommended cruising speed of thirty knots, the Predator only has a range of three hundred nautical miles, the nearest of the Islands is over four hundred and fifty miles away, so they plan to stop in Cartagena to refuel.

The older man is Fernando Castertano, formally of the archaeological museum in Cartagena. He is an expert in Roman archaeology specialising in maritime history. He has been working for Asterion for only a few weeks and is still very excited by the opportunity that Asterion's obvious wealth has created for him to indulge his passion of exploring ancient shipwrecks and not unimportantly, to significantly increase his own wealth. Asterion is paying him very well indeed.

Fernando and Asterion are looking over the charts and the notes that Asterion took from the Madeline.

"Well what do think?" Asterion says.

"She has marked fifteen wreck sites spread equally around Minorca and Majorca. Both islands were on the regular Roman trade routes between Cartagena and Rome and the ship you are looking for may well have passed through the islands. As to why they have selected these sites as candidates, I'm not sure. I'll need to study her notes to work out which of them is the most likely, and then I'll know where we should start our search."

"We will arrive in Cartagena in about eight hours, a couple of hours to refuel than it's a further ten hours to Majorca. I need your recommendation for our first dive site in less than twenty hours, so keep at it," says Asterion.

"That should be possible. I certainly should be able to make an educated guess well before then. What I'm surprised at though, is why that girl left these notes onboard. She knows how much they would help us. Why didn't she take them with her?"

"She knew I tracked her to Cartagena so she needed to get away quickly and quietly. She managed to find passage on the Madeline thinking rightly that I would be informed if she booked tickets on a passenger ship or plane. When the girl saw me on the dock as they were casting off, she knew I'd spotted her and that I would eventually find out where that yacht was going. I think she was frightened and decided to jump ship before they made landfall. She was obviously too worried about her own skin to think about her notes."

Castertano is too shocked by the implications of what Asterion has just said to question the voracity of his reasoning. All he can focus on is the comment, '…too worried about her own skin…' What kind of man is he working for?

Asterion walks towards the door of the saloon and just before he exits, he turns towards Castertano and says. "By the way, I don't pay you to guess. There had better be some good reasons for your choice of wreck. I don't have a high tolerance for failure."

As Asterion turns his back on Castertano and heads towards the bridge to check on their progress towards Cartagena, Castertano returns to studying Adriane's notes and books. The feeling of excitement and anticipation that he was feeling only a few minutes ago has been replaced by a growing unease in his stomach.

7 - GIBRALTAR

It's a relatively short six hour journey from Smir to Gibraltar but Callum and Chloe still get up at dawn so as not to be caught in adverse tidal currents as they cross the eastern end of the Straits of Gibraltar. They pass Europa Point on their starboard side. It is unmistakeable, with its red and white lighthouse and the large white mosque behind it dominating the point. They proceed on into Gibraltar Bay and call ahead to 'Marina Bay-Ocean Village'. It's the most central and largest marina on the Rock and luckily, they have a berth, if only for a couple of days.

As the dockhands direct them to their berth, Callum is convinced they have it wrong. He can't see how even a relatively small boat like the Madeline can be squeezed in between the other boats already moored along the quay. Using their dinghy to nudge a couple of boats apart, the dockhands create a small gap between two of the boats. With bit of help from the dinghy to push the Madeline's bow around, Chloe somehow manages to reverse into the space between the yachts. They knew the marina was going to be a tight squeeze but not this tight. The positive side of being in Gibraltar is the check-in process, unlike Spain or Morocco, it's all done in less than five minutes,

As soon as the boat is secure, they head off to the pub for a drink and to call Val. After months of drinking lager, Callum is relishing the thought of a pint of real ale.

Despite having visited before, they are still surprised at just how British Gibraltar is. Yes, there are there a lot of Spaniards and Moroccans working there, or just visiting for the duty free cigarettes and alcohol, but there is little sign of their cultural influence. Gibraltar is a snapshot of England in the 1960s, just with more sunshine and cheaper booze and cigarettes.

Harry and Val join them for a drink in one of the marina bars. They are very pleased to see them again but are surprised that they are back in Gib so soon after their last visit. Harry and Val are both old sea dogs. They spent much of their early adult life living on boats, even bringing up their children, who never lived permanently ashore until their teens, onboard. They owned and operated one of the few small freighters that did the circuit from Gib to Morocco and back. When Franco closed the border between the Rock and the Spanish mainland in June 1969, these ships were the only way to bring in vital supplies to the British Overseas Territory. When the border reopened in 1985, Harry became a commercial pilot for the boats coming into Gibraltar's port, whereas Val started a new career in the police force. They have both been retired for a few years and split their time between their home in Gibraltar and their children who have moved to the UK.

Harry asks, "What's bought you back to Gibraltar so soon?"

Turning to Val, Chloe answers the question. "We need your advice Val. We've had a couple of strange experiences in the last week or so and don't know what to do. We're afraid that if we report things through official channels, people will think we are mad or lock us up, probably both. If we tell you our story will you promise to keep it between us, unless we all agree that we take it to the authorities?"

"OK, you've got our interest. If what you've done is deliberately illegal, no, I can't promise and I'd rather not know. But if you are in trouble, Harry and I will do everything we can to help," says Val.

Callum and Chloe consider a moment and then decide to continue. They have a lot of respect for both Harry and Val and will trust their judgement. Over a couple of rounds of drinks, they recount the story, starting in Cartagena and finishing with Asterion's visit to the boat in M'diq. Harry and Val ask a few questions along the way, but mostly they listen quietly and attentively to the story.

"Well I can see why you didn't want to report Adriane's disappearance to either the Moroccan or Spanish authorities. Taking on board a complete stranger was frankly stupid. I would have thought you would have known better. She might have been a terrorist, a drug smuggler, or worse. Perhaps she may just have been a naive tourist with no Moroccan visa, who knows. I think that given the circumstances of her disappearance I'm sure she is OK. I agree that you would have got into all sorts of trouble if you reported it in Morocco. If that was the end of the story, I'd say leave it there.

"Your encounter with Asterion is another matter though. He sounds like a nasty piece of work, and if those were police motorcycles escorting the Range Rover, he obviously has some friends in high places. Mmm....." Val pauses in thought for a moment, before continuing.

"I'm not sure reporting this officially will achieve anything positive. Why don't I make some discrete enquiries amongst my old contacts to see what I can find out about Asterion and Adriane," she suggests.

"Thank you, that's what we hoped you'd say," replies Callum.

"I'll leave you in Harry's capable hands for a few hours, while I call in a few favours," says Val as she leaves the table.

"I'm still intrigued as to what Asterion and Adriane are looking for," says Harry. "It's not like you two to leave things hanging like this. If Adriane was trying to misdirect this Asterion chap, it seems to me that the clue to this mystery is in whatever was missing from the notes she left behind for him to find, if you get my drift."

"That's easier said than done," says Callum. "We don't even have her notes anymore."

Harry continues, "Well, let's summarise what we do know then. First, we have a lot of ancient wreck sites marked on charts of the Central Mediterranean. It's probably a fair assumption that they are looking for a particular wreck or something that was on the wreck. Agreed?"

Callum and Chloe both nod in agreement.

"Second, we have two names, Asterion and Francisco Castertano. What do we know of them, anything?"

Callum and Chloe shake their heads. Harry smiles, this is the opportunity he has been waiting for. Reaching into the bag beside him, he takes out his latest purchase.

"We can do a quick google," he says proudly displaying his new iPad Pro tablet. "It's the 128GB Wifi plus Cellular one, mobile hotspot tethering capable, with a 4G Micro SIM and unlimited data contract." He's not sure what it all really means, only that he believed the man in the shop when he said it was the very latest and best, but most importantly for today, he knows it's much more advanced than Callum's iPad.

Never being one to disappoint a good friend, Callum is

really excited by a chance to play with the latest tech. "Wow, can I have a look," says Callum enviously.

"No, not now, we have real work to do, besides you need to have the magic finger," says Harry. He opens his iPad case and swipes his finger over the screen to unlock it. "Didn't I mention the integrated finger print scanner," he says.

Satisfied that Callum is now properly jealous he gets down to business and searches for Asterion. Nothing helpful comes up, but when he searches for Francisco Castertano, he has more luck.

"Castertano was a doctor of Archaeology based at Cartagena Museum in Spain. His doctoral thesis was on Roman shipping, and he is one of the foremost specialists in the field. If he is involved in this, I guess that confirms that we are looking for ancient Roman shipwrecks."

Turning to Callum, Chloe interrupts Harry. "Do you remember the guide in the museum in Cartagena? She took that phone call from the police about a missing colleague. Do you think it could have been him?"

Harry answers before Callum can respond. "Yes I think it might have been. There is a recent newspaper article here about him. I think I can get the gist of the Spanish, but I'll just run it through google translate to be sure."

It takes a Harry a minute or so to get the translation,

Callum, and Chloe wait impatiently for him to continue.

"OK, I think we have our man," says Harry. "There is an appeal here from the head of the museum. He says that a few weeks ago a man came to see Castertano in the office. He stayed for about three hours, after which they both left together. Castertano was in high spirits and told his colleagues that he was taking a few days off. No one has seen sight or sound of him since."

"What do they say about his visitor?" asks Chloe.

"Not a lot, although there is a brief description of him; tall, dark, and spoke in broken Spanish when he first arrived. Once he was introduced to Castertano, they spoke in English and he was very fluent with no trace of an accent. It sounds like it could be Asterion, but also a million other people as well. There's an awful lot of stuff here on roman shipwrecks and Castertano's work, why don't we head back to my flat and see if we can dig out some clues. If we stay in this bar any longer they will have to carry us out."

It's early evening by the time Val joins them in the flat, she has some news as does Harry.

"OK I've got something on Asterion," she says. "He is known to quite a few of the police forces hereabouts. He has never been accused of any specific crime and certainly never been a suspect, but he has been linked to more than a few shady incidents over the years. Apparently, when my colleagues here, in Spain, or the

UK have asked about him officially they are quietly asked to back off and drop their enquiries. When they have asked off the record, there are two schools of thought. One is that he has done the odd favour for some intelligence agencies over the years; the other is that he has bought his influence with some high level payoffs. Anyway, my colleagues have been told 'hands off' unless you have incontrovertible proof of wrongdoing. It certainly could explain why he had the support of the police in Morocco."

"Does he have a surname? Where does he live or operate from?" asks Callum.

"We don't know. However, I think we should steer clear of him. Those shady incidents I mentioned, none of them have been minor. There is no doubt he is a dangerous and powerful man. Leave well alone is my advice," says Val.

"As to making a formal report on what happened to you, we should leave that for now. I think it quite likely that it would get back to Asterion and then he might come looking for you. My old sergeant, who is now an inspector, has made an informal record of the story. If it ever comes up, he will claim that he didn't believe the story and so just sat on it. He will take some flack for that, but at least you will be covered."

"Wow, he must owe you big time to do that," says Chloe.

"Not Val, but me," says Harry, "but that's not a story

we can repeat. Suffice to say we can trust him with this."

"So what have you found out?" asks Val.

Harry fills in Val, telling her that they have identified Castertano and think they have a clue as to where Adriane may actually have gone.

"One of the references we found when researching Castertano and his interest in Roman shipwrecks was this chart of the Mediterranean. It's not one of Castertano's but it looks authoritative enough. As you can see, it has shipwrecks marked all over the Med. On Adriane's charts she circled a number of wrecks on the Balearic Islands."

"Yes, we knew that already," Val replies.

"But if you remember that we now believe Adriane was trying to lay a false trail for Asterion, and if you compare her charts with this one what do you see, or rather don't see?" says Harry.

"Of course the big gap is Sardinia. Your chart shows it was on the major trade routes to Rome and with lots of wrecks. She's sent Asterion to the Balearics while she heads to Sardinia," says Val.

"Exactly what we think," says Chloe. "We're leaving for Sardinia the day after tomorrow. We need to do some provisioning first as it's nearly eight hundred miles from here to Sardinia. We are looking forward to going to Waitrose tomorrow to stock up on some proper British food; baked beans, real beer, teabags, McVities Chocolate Digestives, and most importantly some real English bacon and Heinz Tomato Ketchup. Oh and we've also got to buy a new dinghy, I suspect our old one is on a beach somewhere in Morocco."

"Sheppard's chandlery is the place for that. I'll run you down there in a bit," says Harry.

"We've also promised Harry that we will take you out to your favourite Chinese restaurant in La Linea tomorrow night as a thank you for all your help," says Callum.

"That will be lovely, thanks," says Val. "Hopefully the queues crossing the border won't be too long."

8 - SHIPWRECKED

On the quayside, teams of slaves clad only in breechclouts are struggling to lift heavy ingots of grey metal into the hold of a large wooden cargo ship. The slave master stands above them whip in hand, ready to spur on any slave who might be thinking of taking a momentary break from this heavy labour.

"Hurry along there, get the rest of that cargo loaded we leave at noon," shouts the captain of the large Roman cargo vessel. "That lead is needed in Rome; Caesar's armourers don't like to be kept waiting."

The ship's primary cargo is just over thirty tons of lead ingots from the mines of Gaius and Marcus Pontilienus in Cartagena, Spain, on route to Rome. They are also carrying some amphorae of grain and other goods but the bulk of the large boat is dedicated to the lead.

Atilius Regulus, the captain, is an impressive figure. Tall for a Roman at five foot ten inches he towers over most of the other citizens in the harbour. Dressed in his finest robes he steps down the wooden gangplank and walks through the narrow streets of the harbour heading to the public baths for a meeting with a very important stranger and to collect a special cargo.

Entering the baths through the palaestra, he forgoes the customary bout of exercise and proceeds directly into the apodyterium. He looks across at the other men in the changing room and spots a tall man with a small tattoo on his upper arm, a maze inside a triangle. Almost imperceptibly, he nods at the stranger and removes his street clothes. Atilius proceeds with his bath, first taking a cold plunge in the frigidarium, a short stay in the warmer tepidarium and then into the hottest of bathing rooms, the calidarium. He rubs olive oil into his skin instead of soap to cleanse it, using a curved hook known as a strigil to remove the oil and dirt. As he relaxes in the heat of the hot room, the tall stranger comes across and begins to speak to Atilius.

"My name is Thalius Minosus. You are Captain Atilius Regulus?" he asks.

The captain looks around the room and as no one is paying any attention to them, he briefly raises both his hands and touches his forefingers and thumbs together to form a triangle as he answers the question. Thalius responds to the gesture by drawing a spiral with his forefinger in the air. Having exchanged the correct recognition signs, Thalius gets directly to the business at hand.

"You understand the sensitivity of the cargo you will be carrying for us to Rome. I wish we could send a fleet to protect it but I fear that will only bring it to our enemy's attention sooner. If necessary, we must sacrifice the ship and ourselves to keep it safe. Do you understand and accept these conditions?" he asks.

Slightly offended by the question, the Captain replies, "Of course, I may not be part of the inner circle as are you, but I know what is at stake here. Like you I took the oath and I am prepared to die for the cause."

Head bowed with respect, Thalius responds. "Thank you my friend, I had no doubt that would be your response, but you have the right not to put yourself and your crew at risk, so I had to ask."

In hushed tones, they discuss the route they will take to Rome and the precautions they will take to secure the cargo. Finishing their bath with a final plunge into the frigidarium, they leave the bathhouse. They are met outside by four men and a horse cart carrying a large lead casket. They make their way down to the waterfront and carefully watch the harbour as the casket is loaded onto the boat.

Thalius and the men remain onboard as the final items of cargo are loaded onto the boat and when all is ready, Captain Regulus gives the order to cast off. They enjoy an uneventful voyage towards Rome, stopping off in the Roman port of Tharros on the west coast of the island of Sardinia to re-supply with water and food. Thalius remains on board while Atilius goes ashore to replenish their supplies. The town has grown rapidly since his first visit here some years ago and he is pleased to see it prosper. He notices that the town's third public bathhouse is almost ready to open and looks forward to trying it on the return trip. He concludes the business of re-supplying the boat and returns to the dock, not noticing the trireme on the horizon approaching the bay. Within a few hours, the boat is ready to depart and they set off immediately. Normally they would stop over for a few days to allow the crew some shore leave but the security and importance of their cargo means that this stay is very short.

They have only been at sea for a few hours and have just left the bay, following the coast northwards when they see the trireme rapidly approaching them. Unlike the heavy cargo ship, the trireme is a fast and powerful warship, propelled not only by its two square sails but also by three rows of oarsman, around one hundred and fifty in total. It is capable of cruising all day at around four to five knots and can reach up to eight knots during battle conditions.

The trireme is bearing down on the cargo ship and while the lead is valuable Thalius and Atilius are under no illusions that the ship is after the casket and its contents, not the rest of the cargo. They are too far from Tharros to return even if that would guarantee the safety of the casket, so the captain attempts to outmanoeuvre the trireme around the small island just outside the bay. He is fighting a loosing battle and it is obvious that they will soon be caught. The ship is simply outclassed and his men are outnumbered so Thalius and Atilius regretfully decide to scuttle the ship to keep it and its cargo out of the hands of the enemy.

With the bulk of the island between them and the trireme, such that they have a few minutes in which the enemy cannot see their boat, they throw the casket overboard, after first taking a bearing between the island and the bay. If they manage to escape, they are confident they will be able to find the casket.

In a desperate attempt to save the crew they now drive the ship towards the coast of the island and sink her five or six hundred metres from shore, deep enough that the cargo cannot be retrieved but close enough for the crew to swim to land. The trireme sees the cargo ship sinking and is powerless to stop it. They shoot arrows at the men who are still swimming to shore killing many of them whilst they are still in the water. The enemy land in force on the island and proceed to slaughter all the survivors from the shipwreck with the exception of the captain and Thalius who they take onboard as prisoners.

Thalius and Atilius have been locked up in the small hold of the trireme for at least a day with no food or water. The hold is at the bottom of the boat and they have not been released or spoken to since they were captured. The trireme is taking them for interrogation by its masters. Being an experienced mariner and from the brief glimpses of the sun and the stars he has seen from within their prison cell, the captain can 'feel' their course and approximate speed. He tells Thalius that they are heading towards the Balearic Islands and must now be at least fifty miles from the nearest land.

"I think the time has come Thalius," Atilius says. "If we do it now none of them will survive and the location of the wreck will die with us."

Thalius nods and says, "There are over one hundred and fifty people on this boat. While they are mostly paid mercenaries and soldiers who expect death, they have no idea of what is truly happening here. It saddens me to take their lives this way, with no chance of fighting back like real men."

Atilius reminds Thalius of the importance of their mission and their conversation in the calidarium. "Yes, you are right my friend," agrees Thalius. "It has been an honour to know and serve with you. The stakes are too high to allow this ship to make port and the location of the casket to become known. We must sacrifice them all as well as ourselves."

Removing the clasp that fastens his cloak together, Thalius unscrews the back of the clasp to reveal a small vial of powder. He carefully empties the powder in a line onto the bottom of the hull that they are sitting on. Unscrewing the back of the other side of the clasp, he removes a second vial containing a clear liquid. With a final look and a nod at Atilius, he pours the liquid over the powder and almost immediately, the powder ignites with a brilliant flame burning through the hull of the trireme. The heat is excruciating and Thalius' and Atilius' skin begins to burn. It is a welcome relief when the torrent of water, coming in through the breach in the hull, cools their burning skin, even as it quickly drowns them and sinks the boat.

No living soul survives to reveal the location of the wreck and the casket. They will remain lost for over two thousand years.

9 - SARDINIA ITALY

Callum and Chloe are on their way from Gibraltar to Sardinia, having said goodbye to Harry and Val earlier that morning. They came down to the marina to wave them off and wish them luck with their long passage and their search for Adriane. While this journey is twice the distance of their longest passage so far they are viewing it philosophically. It will be good practice for when they cross the Atlantic to the Caribbean. On that passage they will spend around four weeks at sea something about which they have very mixed feelings.

Under normal circumstances, they would break this journey with a stopover on one of the Balearic Islands, Ibiza, or Minorca but this isn't quite a normal situation, they don't want to run the risk of bumping into Asterion.

The sun is shining, the seas are flat, the wind is blowing at around eighteen knots, and the Madeline is speeding through the water on a beam reach. They are joined by a pod of dolphins that swim alongside and then move up close to the boat where they play in the bow wave for a while. The dolphins stay with them for around thirty minutes and for Callum and Chloe the cares and tensions of the last few days melt away. This is sailing as it should be. They enjoy an uneventful if long passage to Sardinia where they make initial landfall on the west coast at Alghero before heading north and then east to the La Maddalena islands, the sailing ground of the rich and famous as well as the location of a number of ancient shipwrecks.

The La Maddalena islands are a national park and anchoring is only allowed in a few places but the park authorities have laid mooring buoys in the callas (bays) for yachts to tie up to, for a fee of course. Chloe is annoyed that they can't anchor for free in the national park, but at least the buoys are a lot cheaper than the marinas so they secure the Madeline to a buoy, lower the new dinghy, and head off to explore the calla. They are amazed with the clarity and colour of the water, a brilliant turquoise over white sand. They land the dinghy on a secluded beach where they relax for a while, go for a walk, and enjoy a swim. They are very happy to stretch their legs after over a week at sea.

They set off in the dinghy to return to the Madeline but they are hailed from a British sailing boat that has picked up a buoy next to theirs. As always seems to happen with yachties they are invited on board for a drink, which after a few minutes they know will turn into a long night.

"Oh No!" says Callum, "Another assault on our livers coming up."

Chloe smiles and replies, "You love it really."

They all have a fun evening swapping life histories and sailing stories. Soon they are talking as if they have known each other for years. Callum asks their host, Gloria, what her scariest sailing episode has been.

"That's an easy one," she says, "We were at anchor near Cederia in Galicia, Northern Spain. We left the boat and went ashore in the dinghy to explore. As we were walking around the bay, we stopped to take some photos of the boat at anchor. I remember Gordon saying that the change in perspective as we walked around the bay made it look as if the boat had slipped its anchor and had moved. We laughed and continued walking. We walked on for about an hour or so and then had another look across the bay. There was no doubt this time the boat was moving. We were about two miles from the dinghy at this point and I really didn't think I could run that far but somehow I managed it. By the time we got back to the boat she was one hundred yards from the beach with only a few inches of water beneath the keel. A little longer and she would have hit the bottom and fallen over as the tide went out. We nearly lost her that day."

"That's terrible. It's one of my recurring fears," says Callum, "I'm never fully relaxed when we leave the boat at anchor."

"I know exactly what you mean. Neither are we now, but what choice do we have. If we worried about all the things that could go wrong, we'd never have left the UK. Besides, people have been leaving boats at anchor for thousands of years. What's your worst story?" Gordon asks.

Chloe recounts the story of Adriane and their encounter with Asterion. Gloria and Gordon don't believe a word of it but they appreciate a good story. Gloria tells them that they saw a girl answering Adriane's description diving off the back of a large white motor boat near Oristano bay on the west coast last week.

"Perhaps that's where the sunken treasure is," she says with a laugh.

****

Late the next morning, it was another typical yachtie get together and the cheap wine was flowing very freely, they decide to head off to Oristano bay. It's around one hundred and fifty nautical miles so it takes them a few days, as they don't want to sail through the night in these waters. In addition to the many outlying rocks, the seas near the coast are full of the bane of the sailor's life - lobster pots.

The lobster pots laid by fishermen on the sea floor are connected by a long line to a buoy floating on the surface. Some of the buoys have flags and occasionally even a light, but most are simply old twenty gallon plastic containers or a few plastic drinks bottles tied together floating just on the water line. They are very difficult to see even in daylight, virtually impossible at night. The danger for small boats like the Madeline is that you if you don't avoid them, the line will get entangled around the boats propeller or rudder bringing you to a rapid stop. The only way to free the boat is to dive under the boat and cut the line free, not a pleasant task even in the warm waters of the Mediterranean.

When they finally arrive in Oristano bay there is no sign of the large white motor boat Gloria described, but they tie up to a buoy near the wreck site just off the island on Mal di Ventre and the next morning they prepare to dive on the wreck.

They are both certified recreational divers. Callum has a PADI Open Water qualification but Chloe is certified to the much more advanced Master Scuba level so she always leads their dives.

"The wreck is in an average of about fifteen to twenty five metres of water. If we swim no deeper than eighteen metres, our maximum 'no decompression limit' is fifty six minutes. So we should be able to stay over the wreck for around forty minutes, and then come up to five metres for our safety stop, before surfacing. Watch your air and don't forget to tell me when your air level is down to one hundred bar," says Chloe.

Callum knows all this, but just nods to show he understands. They put on their wet suits, BCDs and other dive gear. After checking that each other's equipment has been set up correctly, Chloe resets the dive computer on her wrist and then one after the other; they take a giant stride off the stern of the Madeline into the water.

The water here isn't quite as clear as in the La Maddalena islands but the visibility is still very good and they swim on the surface until they are above the main part of the wreck, where they slowly descend equalising pressure in their ears as they go down. The wreck is an old one; around two thousand years old encrusted in barnacles but mostly clear of seaweed. They see that the wreck had been systematically excavated and explored by other divers since it was first discovered and that is why most of the weed has been removed and hence it is relatively easy to see. Even allowing for the fact that the boat would have broken up as it sank and spread out on the seabed before it was covered with silt, it's readily apparent that this was a very large ship for the time.

What really astonishes them, is not the size or the remarkably good condition of the wreck, it's the cargo. Not just the usual ceramic amphorae filled with oil and grain or chests full of trade goods but ingots of metal. Much of the cargo has been recovered but some has been left undisturbed on the wreck. Chloe's dive computer on her wrist beeps, its time for them to begin to surface as they are reaching the maximum amount of time they can safely spend at this depth.

Back on the surface, they are both perplexed.

"Well, we must have got that wrong," says Callum. "There is nothing there that would have been of interest to treasure hunters and even if there was it would have been found by now. It's obvious that that boat has been dived hundreds if not thousands of times."

They surface swim back to the Madeline. Callum removes his fins and passes them to Chloe. With his BCD and air tank still on his back, he struggles with the weight as he slowly hauls himself up the swim ladder to get onboard. After he has removed his gear, Chloe passes both sets of fins to Callum. As Chloe starts to climb the swim ladder Callum reaches down to take the weight of her tank making it much easier for her to get onboard.

"Sailing, diving, skiing, why don't we take up tiddlywinks or something, anything that doesn't involve expensive clothing or lugging heavy gear around," Callum says a little breathlessly.

Chloe laughs, "What are you moaning about. I didn't find it at all hard to get back onboard. Man up princess," she jokes as she kisses him affectionately.

Callum kisses her back.

They decide to head into Oristano bay and anchor near Torre Grande marina so they can take the dinghy ashore to refill their air tanks at the local dive shop.

While they are waiting for the bottles to be filled, it will take a while as the dive shop was just shutting for the usual three-hour Italian lunch break, they head to a bar for a beer and to use the wifi.

Callum takes out his iPad mini and starts to research the wreck. It was discovered in 1988 and was one of the Roman's largest class of cargo vessel, known simply in Latin as a 'navis oneraria magna' or big cargo boat. It measured thirty six meters in length and twelve meters wide. In addition to amphorae of grain and oil it's primary cargo was around two thousand lead ingots weighing around thirty nine tons from the mines in Cartagena and was on route to Rome. The archaeologists who have extensively studied the wreck could find no evidence of what caused it to sink, no sign of fire, or it being crushed on rocks or by big waves. The archaeologists speculate that the captain deliberately scuttled the ship to keep it out of enemy hands.

"Nothing to attract treasure hunters here," says Callum.

Chloe agrees and adds that Gloria and Gordon must have seen someone else here, not Adriane. They return to the dive shop to collect their tanks, the owner who speaks good English asks them where they are intending to dive next.

"We've just dived on the wreck of the big Roman ship off Mal di Ventre, but don't have another dive site in mind yet. Can you recommend one around here?" Callum asks.

"Yes Mal di Ventre, it means Stomach Ache Island

you know, is one of the most popular dive sites here," he says as he goes onto to describe a number of other sites showing them pictures of the sea life and a few look interesting. Just as they are about to leave he adds.

"A few weeks ago a very large white motorboat moored out by the island for a few days. They did one or two dives on the wreck but the rest of the time, they seemed to be working a line heading northeast about a kilometre from the wreck. I've been meaning to go out and see what they found but the shop has been too busy and at this time of year, I'm constantly running PADI courses. If you fancy an adventure, check it out and let me know what you find. Also, if you have the time you should really go and check out the museum in Cabras. A lot of the artefacts recovered from the wreck are displayed there."

"I think you might need to apologise to Gloria and Gordon," says Callum as they leave the dive shop.

"I hope so," says Chloe.

They return in the dinghy to the Madeline and decide to move the boat and pick up a buoy just off the ruins of the Roman town of Tharros in the NW corner of the bay. The next day they visit the ruins and are impressed by the size of the ancient town. As they sit and eat a picnic lunch by one of the three roman baths, they ponder the conversations and secrets the walls could recount if they could only talk. After lunch, they take a taxi journey into the small town of Cabras that is only a few miles away. They are stunned by the display of perfectly preserved lead ingots and amphorae recovered from the wreck.

Callum in particular is fascinated by the display panels that describe how some of the antique lead has been used as shielding in an international physics experiment, CUORE, to detect neutrino decay rates. It doesn't have the low-level background radioactivity of freshly mined lead and so it significantly improves the sensitivity of the experiment. Chloe isn't quite sure what that really means but she is very disappointed that they have gained no further insight into whatever Adriane was looking for.

They return to Tharros, board the dinghy and head back to the Madeline. It's been a busy day and they are exhausted. Callum quickly knocks up some chicken and sweet corn pasta with pesto for their dinner and they sit in the cockpit to eat it, with the almost obligatory glass of wine. The sun won't be setting for a few hours yet, but even without the sunset, the evening is beautiful. There are no other boats on the buoys today and the tourists have left the ruins at Tharros.

They are alone in one of the most spectacular bays of their sailing career. The sea is a deep turquoise and the hills a magnificent green framing the Roman ruins only a few hundred yards away on the shore. As the sun sets and the colours darken and then fade into the night, they reflect on how privileged and lucky they are to live this way.

****

The next day they return to the island of Mal di Ventre and from the dinghy attempt to follow the line suggested by the dive shop owner. The water here is quite shallow between less than ten to twenty metres and in the crystal clear waters they can clearly see the seabed, which for the most part is covered by posidonia sea grass.

The grass is an essential part of the local ecosystem, acting as a fish nursery and is an important natural defence against coastal erosion. Consequently, it's protected by law and boats are not allowed to anchor on it. So Callum and Chloe are surprised to see a number of disturbed areas of seabed where the grass has been deliberately cut down. These are all in a line running northeast from the wreck. They return to the Madeline for their dive gear and then return to the last patch in the line. This is obviously the last place Adriane must have dived.

After deploying a sea anchor from the dinghy, they suit up and after completing their buddy checks, they do a backward roll off the sides of the dinghy into the water.

Back under the water, in the centre of the disturbed area of grass they come across a very old, empty, lead casket. It's been forced open. The inside of the casket which is completely clear of any marine growth, contains a cradle for a long cylindrical object. The lack of marine growth implies that the casket had been opened very recently. Looking at the cradle, they estimate that the casket contained a cylindrical object around four to five inches in diameter and two feet long. They examine the outside of the casket and Callum closes the lid. A section of the lid has been scraped clean to reveal two carvings, one of a man with a bulls head and the other a maze inside a triangle. They take some photos of the casket with their underwater camera and they continue to search the area until its time to surface.

Onboard the Madeline, Callum, and Chloe are discussing what to do next. They are now certain that Adriane was here, had dived on the wreck, and removed something from the casket. The only clue they have as to where to go to next, are the two carvings on the lid of the casket.

"A Man with a bulls head and a maze implies the Minotaur and the Labyrinth. That suggests Crete, but I'm not sure what the triangle is about though?" says Chloe.

"Yes, the triangle could be anything but I agree about the other two. It can't really be anything else. The Greek islands were always part of our plan," says Callum, "and we have to begin our tour of them somewhere, so it might as well be there. It will take a week or two to get to Crete so we should get started. I wonder what our best route is."

"Head to the south of Sardinia, cross to Scilly and then

direct to Crete," says Chloe confidently. Callum agrees, but fully intends to work out a more detailed passage plan before they cast off from the buoy.

****

It's a week or so later and back in Minorca; Asterion has just surfaced after exploring the third wreck marked on Adriane's charts. Never a patient man he is becoming increasingly frustrated and angry by the lack of success. After removing his dive gear, and still dripping wet, he moves into the saloon of his powerboat, which although slightly smaller than the Minos is still luxurious and impressive. Oblivious to effect the saltwater dripping off him is having on the carpet and soft furnishings, he bellows at the middle-aged man sitting at a desk covered in books and charts.

"Castertano, again nothing! If you don't get it right soon you will be swimming back to Cartagena."

Francisco Castertano is beginning to regret agreeing to help Asterion. When he came to the museum in Cartagena looking for help in tracking down an ancient shipwreck, Asterion seemed charming and cultured. The half million euros he offered to entice him to immediately abandon his work at the museum and join the search was too large to refuse and he quickly put aside any misgivings he had about the legality of Asterion's activities. However, after spending over a month on the search he has realised the man is not only unstable but also probably dangerous. From his most recent review of Adriane's notes he has come to a conclusion and isn't quite sure how to tell Asterion.

Taking a deep breath Castertano begins. "I think someone is trying to distract and delay us."

Asterion stops in mid stride and his already black expression darkens even further as Castertano keeps on talking.

"All but one of the wreck sites we have dived so far have been an ancient warship, not the large cargo vessel you are looking for. They are all so deep and widely spaced around the islands that it would take months or years to properly check them all. It's almost as if someone selected the hardest ones to search."

Seeing Asterion's anger rise he quickly continues hoping to present his conclusions before Asterion explodes. "What's just struck me is that there are no wrecks marked in Sardinia at all and that island was on the trade route from Cartagena to Rome. The ship we are looking for would almost certainly have stopped there."

Asterion considers his words for a moment, his anger visibly subsides, and his face lights up for the first time in a month.

"By the gods!" he exclaims. "How simple the trick and I fell for it. Castertano, you have done well, I will double your fee," he says as he heads off to the bridge to order the captain to head for Sardinia.

Castertano is perplexed by Asterion's sudden change of mood and he wanders about what could be so valuable to warrant all this effort and his now one million euro fee. His concerns melt away as he dreams about the comfort and opportunities his hopefully now imminent wealth will buy him.

****

On arrival in Sardinia, not knowing where to start the search for the wreck or for Adriane, Asterion leaves Castertano to continue working through the literature on ancient shipwrecks and Roman settlements in Sardinia. He goes ashore for some old fashioned detective work. Working his way through the port bars and marinas on the island, he and his agents are asking if anyone has seen the Madeline or Adriane.

After a few days, he is overheard talking to a barman by Gordon and Gloria. Gloria interrupts the conversation and says that she might have some information of interest. Holding up her empty glass, she waits for Asterion to take the hint before she continues. Ignoring the look of concern on her husband's face Gloria tells Asterion that she saw a large white Sunseeker motorboat putting divers down near Oristano Bay, one of which matched his description of Adriane."

"When was this?" Asterion asks the excitement and control in his voice very clear even to Gloria who has been drinking all afternoon. Asterion motions to the barman who refills her glass. Gloria tells him that the motorboat stayed in the bay for about four days then left.

As Asterion leaves Gordon turns to Gloria, "You shouldn't have said anything to him, he could have been that guy in Morocco."

"Don't be so stupid," says Gloria. "I didn't believe a word of that yarn and neither did you at the time. Ordinary people being kidnapped and held at gunpoint; that kind of thing only happens on the telly or in books."

Gordon sighs and turns back to his drink that is now sticking in his throat.

****

Asterion returns to his boat and tells Castertano to check out wreck sites in Oristano Bay. He quickly comes across a record of the cargo ship and explains that it has been systematically searched and excavated by teams of divers over recent years. Asterion is convinced it's the ship they are looking for.

"Obviously if the casket was on board it would have been found years ago. A find like that would certainly have been reported internationally, it's obviously not there," he says.

"So what exactly are we looking for?" asks Castertano.

"The key to great riches and power," Asterion replies

but he does not offer any further information. "I suspect that the professor and his daughter would have found and removed any clues that may be there by now. I don't see any point in searching that wreck. We need to get to Crete as soon as possible."

"Why Crete?" asks Castertano.

Ignoring the question Asterion says. "Castertano, I suggest you spend the next few days brushing up on your ancient Greek language and myths."

10 - CRETE

Onboard the Madeline Callum and Chloe are making good progress and will be arriving in Crete shortly. At their current speed, they will arrive around three in the morning so to avoid the dangers of entering an unfamiliar port in the dark, they slow down so that they will arrive after dawn, in daylight. Callum has been researching the legend of the Minotaur and he summarises the story for Chloe.

"It's the usual story of power, lust, and manipulative petulant gods," he begins. "The story starts with King Minos who fought with his brothers for the right to rule Crete. Minos prayed to Poseidon, the god of the sea for a sign that he was the favoured candidate and asked him to send him a snow-white bull. He was meant to kill the bull to show honour to Poseidon, but because it was so rare and beautiful, he decided to keep it for himself. He thought Poseidon would not care if he kept the white bull and sacrificed one of his own instead."

"Doesn't sound like a very bright move to me," says Chloe.

"No it wasn't," continues Callum. "To punish Minos, Poseidon made Pasiphae, Minos' wife, fall in love with the bull. Pasiphae was so desperate to sleep with the bull that she had Daedalus the engineer and architect make a hollow wooden cow that she climbed into so she could couple with the white bull. She got pregnant and the child was the Minotaur.

"The child had the head and tail of a bull but the body of a man. The myths say that even though initially the queen breast-fed him, the Minotaur could not eat normal food and had to eat human flesh to survive. It caused such terror and destruction on Crete that this time Minos summoned Daedalus and ordered him to build a gigantic, intricate labyrinth from which escape would be impossible. The Minotaur was captured and locked in the labyrinth.

"Meanwhile Minos had just won a war of revenge against the Athenians for the killing of his son Androgeus. Minos demanded that every year for nine years, seven youths, and seven maidens came as tribute from Athens. These young people were sent into the labyrinth for the Minotaur to eat.

"When the Greek hero and prince of Athens, Theseus learned of the Minotaur and the sacrifices, he was outraged and wanted to put an end to the tributes. He volunteered to go to Crete masquerading as one of the victims. Upon his arrival in Crete, he met Ariadne, Minos' and Pasiphae's daughter, who fell in love with him. If he agreed to marry her, she promised she would provide the means to escape from the labyrinth.

He did so and she gave him a large ball of string that he was to fasten close to the entrance of the maze. Theseus made his way through the maze unwinding the string as he went and eventually found the sleeping Minotaur. He killed it and led the other tributes out by following the string."

"Interesting times," says Chloe. "Minos and his wife sound like a right pair, but it seemed that Theseus' heart was in the right place."

"I'm not so sure," says Callum. "On his way back to Athens, Theseus abandoned Ariadne on the island of Naxos and continued on without her. He had told his father, King Aegeus of Athens, that if he was successful in killing the Minotaur he would raise a white sail as opposed to the black one his ship usually carried. However he didn't do this and the king assuming that Theseus was dead killed himself in despair, securing the throne of Athens for Theseus."

"Lovely people these ancient Greeks weren't they. I know we can visit the ruins of Minos' palace at Knossos when we get to Crete but what about the labyrinth?" asks Chloe.

"I think it's difficult to judge Theseus," replies Callum. "These people lived in very different times. There are so many conflicting versions of the myth and the lives of the principal players, so I really wouldn't like to say. But hey, these are legends; these people never really existed did they? As to the palace and the maze,

Knossos is there but as far as I can make out there is no archaeological record of anything that could be the labyrinth."

They carry on talking into the evening until its time for them to start taking watches through the night. The following morning they anchor in a bay on the north east coast of Crete near Kissamos, where they rest for a day and enjoy a glass or two of the local 'grasin' (wine) before proceeding to Heraklion from where they can visit the ruined palace complex of Knossos.

****

Adriane and the professor are enjoying a glass of vintage Bollinger in the air conditioned salon of the Minos. They are at anchor in a small bay on the south coast of the small island of Dia, about seven miles north of Heraklion.

"I still find it difficult to believe that after two thousand years in the water, the casket containing the Keystone hadn't leaked and that it appears to be in perfect working order," remarks Adriane.

"Our forebears built to last and in many ways their technology was much more advanced than that we have at present. In fact I suspect that there are very few areas where modern science is ahead, but in a couple of days we will know," replies the professor.

On the table in front of them is the Keystone, a golden cylinder one side of which is adorned with seven jewelled buttons each marked with a short inscription in the Greek alphabet. On the other side is a set of inscriptions in the same language. The language bears a strong resemblance to ancient Greek but is sufficiently different that it has taken Professor Theos weeks of constant work to decipher it.

The inscriptions on the Keystone describe how to locate the entrance to the Labyrinth and of the trials, you will need to pass through to reach its centre. Theos is physically and emotionally exhausted after working almost twenty-four hours a day to decipher the inscriptions, but his dark brown eyes are sparkling with anticipation and excitement.

It's been so very long," he says, "And now we are nearly there. Tomorrow we will find the entrance to the Labyrinth and then hopefully, if we prove ourselves worthy, we will reach the Cornucopia and the Index."

Adriane too is optimistic, but she worries about the trials they will face. Will they complete them successfully and survive?

"I think its time to get a good night's sleep. We should get an early start tomorrow," she says as she walks to the table and picks up the Keystone. She places it in a padded aluminium cylindrical case and moves to a large mural depicting the palace of King Minos at Knossos on the wall. She swings the painting from the wall, which hinges on the left hand side to reveal a large safe into which she places the cylinder. As she finishes her glass of vintage champagne she bids her father goodnight.

"Please don't stay up too late and try to get a good night's sleep," she says as she heads to her cabin.

****

Callum and Chloe are visiting the ruins of the palace complex at Knossos. They have spent the whole day there, talking to the guides and curators at the museum looking for a clue as to what Adriane and Asterion were after. Callum is disappointed to learn that what they saw at Knossos is largely the creation of the 1920's archaeologist Arthur Evans. In an attempt to preserve the remaining archaeology, Evans restored, Callum thinks over restored, much of the palace complex using modern materials. Callum is convinced that Evans attempted to recreate Knossos faithfully, but it's clear that much of what he did was based on his knowledge of similar buildings and his imagination, not just what was on the ground.

Despite this they are both fascinated by the site, especially the sophistication of the complex's water system. It had three separate systems that ran through much of it. One carried fresh water into the buildings, a second carried rainwater runoff and a third wastewater. At its height Knossos housed a population of around one hundred thousand people.

While they have enjoyed their visit to the site, they haven't made any progress in finding Ariadne. They decide to stop in a beachside bar for a drink before returning to the Madeline.

In the bar, they get talking to a German couple, Hans and Andrea who are holidaying on the island. Hans in particular is struggling to understand their lifestyle.

"So what do you with yourselves every day? I can see the attraction for a few days or perhaps a week or two, but you must be really bored most of the time. And you obviously had such good jobs, you gave up so much. How do you manage with so much less?"

Chloe is little taken aback by how quickly and directly Hans asks the question that most people have when they first hear about their lifestyle. But she can see that there is no malice in his question, just a genuine interest and a desire to understand a little more of what to him is a completely alien way of life.

"You mean how do we manage for money," Chloe says. "Well when we sold our home we invested in some smaller properties that give us a modest income. It's a fraction of what we used to earn, but we are managing OK. Living on the boat is very cheap in comparison to running a house in England. We don't pay Council Tax…" Hans raises his eyebrows questioningly so Chloe explains. "Council Tax is the tax we pay to our local or regional government, not to the national government in London. Our water and electricity is usually included in our mooring fees and we don't have the expense of running cars or commuting to work. We live mostly in shorts and tshirts so we spend very little on clothes, and of course, we don't have to pay for holidays. Even when we include the cost of maintaining the boat, our outgoings are a small fraction of what we spent in the UK."

"But surely you spend a lot in bars and restaurants," Hans says.

"We eat out whenever we want to, usually lunch when we are out exploring and of course we visit the odd bar or two, but we eat and drink a lot on board as well. If truth were told, we quickly get bored with the restaurants. We can usually decide what we are going to eat before we see the menu. There just isn't the variety of cuisine that we are used to in England. On the other hand, the restaurants and bars are usually much cheaper than at home, so that's good. Yes, we can't afford many drinks in the more upmarket resorts, but in truth we don't miss that."

Before Hans can enquire further into their finances, Andrea decides it would be polite to change the subject and asks Callum to answer the first part of her husband's question.

"We are far to busy to get bored," Callum says. "Boats are just not that reliable so there is always something to fix, sometimes it's a major problem but mostly it's lots of little things. Even the most popular modern boats are only built in relatively small numbers, a few hundred or a few thousand. With cars, they make so many that the manufacturers can invest in lots of testing and quality even on the cheapest cars. Boats though are still largely hand built using components that are simply not as well developed. When you take an older boat like ours, only around one hundred and fifty of her were ever built, they will always need looking after.

"But that's only part of it. We move around a lot, so each time we go shopping we need to work out where the market or the shops are and how to get there. It's always an adventure and it takes a long time. Either we walk, cycle – we have folding bikes onboard - or get a bus. On the whole we don't miss having a car"

Chloe adds to Callum's answer, "Of course it's not all about doing the domestic stuff. We've become professional tourists, there is always a lot to see, and while we need a break occasionally, we are still excited by every place we visit. We also have the time to do the things we've always wanted to do. Callum is learning the guitar and is planning to write a book, and I'm learning to paint. Watercolours are my thing at the moment. But enough about us, how are you enjoying Crete," she asks.

Hans and Andrea tell them of their travels around Crete and how yesterday, they took a day trip to the island of Dia, which they thought was stunningly pretty. After a final drink, they say their goodbyes and go their separate ways.

****

It's a beautiful evening and Callum and Chloe are sat

in the cockpit watching the sunset and drinking a glass of Crete's finest 'grasin', purchased that evening in the local supermarket, a five litre plastic cask for eight euros.

"That was a beautiful sunset," says Callum. "But the stars would be so much brighter if we weren't so close to town. What do you say to heading off tomorrow to find somewhere a little more secluded? From Andrea's description Dia sounded lovely."

Chloe readily agrees, for her nights at anchor in quiet bays are one of the high spots of their lifestyle.

11 - DIA

It's early morning. Adriane and her father are on the swim platform of the Minos and they are climbing into its tender to go ashore. As you would expect it's a little bigger than the Madeline's dinghy. Nearly five metres in length with a solid floor the RIB or rigid inflatable boat, is driven to shore by Ellie who sets them down on a small sandy beach. Leaving them on the beach with a couple of large backpacks and the cylindrical aluminium carrying case containing the Keystone, Ellie heads off to Heraklion to purchase some fresh food for the Minos' kitchen.

Dia is a small island of around four and a half square miles. It is now uninhabited but is visited regularly by tripper boats, bringing tourists from Heraklion ashore to enjoy its beaches for the day. In the evenings, when the day boats leave, the island is deserted apart from the odd yacht at anchor enjoying the solitude. Once heavily wooded, the trees were cut down in ancient times to supply the shipbuilders of its now ruined and sunken harbour. The harbour was destroyed by the tsunami resulting from the big volcanic eruption and earthquake at Thera (modern day Santorini) in around 1450 B.C.

Theos and Adriane have completed a slow climb up the steep cliffs from the beach and are walking north into the centre of the island. It has taken most of the day to locate the entrance to the Labyrinth. The instructions on the Keystone as to how to find the entrance were very clear, but of course, the landscape has changed a lot in the two thousand years since the inscriptions were added to the Keystone. They have made more than one wrong turn today but finally they have arrived. Ahead of them is a bare and unremarkable small hill.

On the west side of the hill there is a small cave, really not much more than an indentation in the rock about five or six feet deep. They remove a couple of small axes from their backpacks and proceed to clear away the bushes that obstruct the rear wall. It's hard and thirsty work under the hot Cretan sun. It takes the remainder of the afternoon, but by the time the sun begins to set, they have finally cleared the cave and dragged the remains of the bush clear. Adriane takes her father's hand and they both turn to face the back wall of the cave.

"If we didn't know this was the entrance to the Labyrinth you would definitely never guess. Are you sure this is the right place father?" says Adriane.

"The instructions on the Keystone were quite explicit and I'm sure we are in the right place. Remember it was designed as a secret entrance by one of the best engineers of his time. If there was any sign of a doorway, I would have been disappointed and worried," he replies. "Remove the Keystone and give it a try."

The rays of the setting sun are almost horizontal and can now reach the back of the cave, lighting up the rear wall. Adriane releases her father's hand and retrieves the aluminium cylindrical case that she carefully placed on the ground behind them. She opens the case and passes the Keystone to her father.

"Here father, the honour should be yours, after all you deciphered the inscriptions," she says.

Theos shakes his head and almost choked with emotion he says, "No, daughter you are my heir, please go ahead."

Following her fathers instructions, Adriane presses one of the jewelled buttons on the Keystone and then another. For a moment, nothing happens, but suddenly there is a fall of dust as the rock wall in front of them seems to dissolve into thin air. Behind the dust they can see a portal, around ten feet high and just wide enough for two people to walk through side by side. Through the portal, they see a long steep stone stairway descending steeply into the heart of the island.

They smile at each other and then Adrianne quickly moves to hold her father as the emotion of the moment makes him go weak at the knees and he slowly crumples to the ground.

"It's getting late. We should be fully rested before we enter the Labyrinth. I think we need to be at our best to pass the trials ahead."

Her father agrees and adds, "We should also bring Ellie. I suspect we will need her skills down there as well."

Adrianne presses the first symbol again and the portal vanishes.

****

After a leisurely breakfast of fresh fruit, Greek yoghurt and honey, Callum and Chloe have raised the anchor and are motoring across to Dia in search of a quiet anchorage away from the bustle and lights of Heraklion. Forewarned by the trip ashore yesterday they aren't too disheartened to find the bays full of day boats, knowing that come the evening most would have returned to Crete. They drop anchor on the same side of the bay as the Minos that is around five hundred metres away. Entranced by the beauty of the island and the crystal clear water, they don't immediately connect the big white motor boat with Adriane.

Ellie is returning from her shopping trip to Heraklion, in the RIB. She spots the Madeline at anchor and immediately realises who they are. Coming to a quick decision, she diverts to the Madeline and engages Callum who is on deck working on their dinghy's outboard motor in conversation.

"Hi there, is everything OK? Do you need a run ashore?"

"That's very kind, but no thanks, just doing a bit of routine maintenance," replies Callum. "On that RIB you must be from that big white motor boat."

"Yes, but I only work there. I crew for the professor and his daughter," replies Ellie.

Chloe who has been listening has now come up from down below and being a bit sharper and faster than her husband says to Ellie. "You mean Adriane don't you."

Ellie nods. After a few more minutes of conversation Ellie suggests that they come aboard the Minos and surprise Adriane and her father who are due to return from the island in a little while. Callum & Chloe readily agree. They invite Ellie aboard for a few minutes while Callum finishes with the outboard. After cleaning themselves up a bit, they close and lock the hatches on the boat and climb aboard the RIB with Ellie.

On the Minos Ellie gives them a quick tour of the boat making sure that she doesn't leave them alone in the library. In addition to the painting of King Minos' palace, the walls are covered in a number of pictures portraying Ariadne and Theseus. The faces in these portraits are all very different and date from the fifteenth to twentieth century, but all are obviously depicting the two classical characters. They are in the library just long enough for Callum and Chloe to take in the paintings, the Greek texts and the charts. They now have no doubt that they are back on the trail.

Ellie leaves the Williamses on the skydeck while a white clad steward brings them a glass of the vintage Bollinger and canapés. He leaves the bottle in a silver ice bucket on the polished mahogany bar, making it clear that they are free to help themselves to more if they want it.

As the steward leaves, Callum turns to his wife, "One up on a cask of our local 'grasin' and a few olives, don't you think?" he says.

Chloe nods in appreciation "Treasure hunters, if that's what they are, must make a very tidy living," she replies.

They drink slowly, but the bottle soon empties and the steward quietly replaces it with another.

****

Meanwhile Ellie has had a call from the Professor and is just collecting them from the beach where she dropped them off earlier that day.

"We have some visitors aboard," she says as she points out the Madeline to the professor and Adriane. "I thought it best to invite them aboard where we can keep an eye on them, rather than have them wandering around like loose canon. It might just be coincidence that they are here, but I suspect they may have followed our trail and we certainly don't want them attracting unwanted attention at this late stage."

"I think you did the right thing Ellie, well done," replies the professor. "Let's talk to them and see what they know."

Adriane interrupts and says, "Remember that we involved them in this father and if they followed us here it's because of me and you. They deserve to be treated fairly."

Theos is a bit put out by the tone of Adriane's comment. "Of course, if they are the innocents they appear to be, they deserve our respect and thanks. We must never forget who we are and what we stand for," he says.

"My apologies father, I spoke harshly and did not mean to offend," replies Adriane with her head bowed in genuine respect and regret for questioning her father's integrity.

The dinghy approaches the Minos and Ellie manoeuvres it to the swim platform on the stern. One of the crew ties on the dinghy's painter and the professor and Adriane quickly freshen up before going to greet their guests.

12 - THE END OF THE TITANS

The Williamses have moved into the Minos' main saloon to avoid the ever present mosquitoes on the island. Chloe has been thinking, her brain cells stimulated by the glasses of fine champagne she has been given. The family obsession with ancient Greek history, the references to the Minotaur, the name of the boat and the artefacts in the library are all suddenly very suggestive. She now believes that the portraits are of real people from the last five hundred years, not representations of the classical Ariadne and Theseus painted over the last five hundred years.

Theos and Adriane enter the saloon.

Not drunk but emboldened by the champagne, Chloe gets up and walks to the door to greet them. She shakes the professor by the hand and stressing the names carefully says, "Thank you very much for your hospitality Theseus," and turning to the girl says, "We were very worried about you out there on the coast of Morocco, Ariadne, but I see you are quite OK." Callum notices his wife's use of the names, it takes a second or two but Callum eventually catches up with his wife's thinking.

Ariadne smiles and looks at her father who gives her a barely perceptible nod and then she says to Chloe "Well done! I always had you down as the smart one Chloe. If you let me fix us all a drink, I'll explain it all."

Ariadne pours herself and her father a glass of champagne, tops up the other two and is about to start telling her tale.

Theseus interrupts Ariadne's flow before she can begin. Turning to Callum he asks, "You managed to find us so I guess you know why we are here in Crete. I'm interested in hearing how you found us."

Callum starts with their encounter with Asterion in Morocco, their visit to Gibraltar and then explains how through a mix of deduction and luck they followed the trail to Sardinia and then Crete. "After we got to Knossos the trail really went cold. We only came across to Dia to get away from the crowds, so again it was blind luck or fate that directed us to find you. However, you are wrong professor, we really don't know why we are here. It's obvious you and Asterion are searching for something but we don't know what. I'm pretty certain you're not run of the mill treasure hunters."

"No we're not, but we are searching for treasure of a sort," says Ariadne. "Father, I think I can proceed now don't you?" Without giving him a chance to respond Ariadne continues, "Now if we are all sitting comfortably, I'll begin," she says.

****

"This will be a long story and it begins a long time ago. A few thousand years before the rise of the Ancient Greek Civilisation in the Mediterranean, there existed a small race of people. They were long lived, with natural life spans of many hundreds of years but very few survived long enough to die of old age. They thrived on conflict and constantly fought amongst themselves for control of their civilisation and their subject (slave) races, our Greek ancestors. As their technology advanced, they became better at killing each other and this coupled with a naturally low birth rate meant that their numbers dwindled to the point at which the race was dying out. It wasn't many long until they were vastly outnumbered by their slaves. Despite their greater intelligence and technology, they could no longer effectively control them. The slave races eventually formed their own civilisation of city states centred on the domains and estates of their old masters.

"Most of these Ancients, led by a man history remembers as Zeus and his Olympians saw the Greeks and the peoples of the Mediterranean as their playthings. No longer battling amongst themselves, at least for the most part, the Olympians focused their love of conflict on the Greeks using them as proxies to fight their own battles, just like pawns in a giant game of chess.

"However not all of the Ancients were cruel and bloodthirsty, a small group led by Zeus' father, a man the legends remember as Cronus, wanted to help the Greeks and he fought to temper the excesses of the Olympians. But Cronus and his Titans were eventually defeated by the far larger Olympian fraction of the Ancients.

"In what was literally a titanic series of battles Zeus killed his father, Cronus, and most of his followers. The few surviving Titans and some of their human allies scattered and fled, living in anonymity amongst the Greeks doing what they could to help and support them."

Callum and Chloe who always enjoy a good yarn are enthralled but very sceptical.

"A nice story and I can see a few parallels with the Greek myths, but it doesn't quite fit," says Callum.

"Yes it's quite surprising that the oral histories Homer documented in 850 BC and by others that followed him even got a fraction of the real story right. You should remember that they were writing about events that happened many hundreds of years before they were born. And as you know, the victor always rewrites history and Zeus made the Titans out to be bloodthirsty power crazed despots. Eating your children as infants and then regurgitating them many years later as fully-grown adults, these can only be stories to scare the children," says Theseus as he buzzes a steward on the intercom.

Before Callum can respond, the steward enters and the professor asks him to prepare dinner for the four of them.

"Please bear with us, I think you will believe and understand by the time we get to desert," Ariadne says with a disarming smile and continues with her story.

"In an attempt to save the race and boost their birth rate the Olympians cross bred with their subjects. Most of the unions did little more than satisfy the warped carnal desires of the Olympians, but a few were fruitful and some of the names are still remembered today as the demigods of ancient Greece, Heracles, Achilles, Dionysus, and others. The remaining Titans took a different path. They focused on preserving the knowledge of the Ancients and they worked to temper the excesses of the Olympians.

"You will know from the legends that the Minotaur was the offspring of the Cretan Bull and Queen Pasiphae, herself the half-breed offspring of the Olympian Helios. The Minotaur's father was actually Poseidon, the brother of Zeus, not a mythical bull. The child initially looked normal but as he grew it became clear that something was wrong. The child was huge with an outsized head and thick limbs. Poseidon took him from his mother and he spent his first few years on Mount Olympus. His outsized head housed a huge intellect; in fact, he was probably the most intelligent being to have lived on Earth up until that time or perhaps since. He quickly surpassed his teachers on Olympus and he was soon dramatically extending the Olympians' already advanced knowledge.

"Unfortunately for him, the mutation that accelerated his metabolism and was also the cause of his great size and intellect, was also killing him. Instead of inheriting the two hundred year plus lifespan of his father, he would be lucky to make four decades. He left his home on Olympus and went to his birthplace on Crete to try to find a way to increase his lifespan.

With the help of his mother Pasiphae and the engineer Daedalus he created an underground laboratory. He laboured away in the laboratory for many years. Driven and twisted by the realisation that he only had a handful of years to live and with a moral compass set by the 'gods' on Olympus, he had no scruples on how he might achieve his goals.

"It was abhorrent, but he used live human subjects as guinea pigs in his researches and trials. Initially he raided the local villages to get his subjects, but King Minos having just won a war with Athens demanded tribute from them. Every year Athens sent fourteen young men and women to Crete. Minos sent these tributes to a gruesome death into the Labyrinth where the Minotaur used them in his experiments.

"The last few surviving Titans were appalled at what was happening. Not only at the callous disregard of human life, but also at what might happen to the rest of the human race if the Minotaur was successful in extending his life and halting the decline of the Olympians. So these surviving Titans led by one of their offspring, Theseus, who was at this time masquerading as a prince of Athens, volunteered to be a tribute.

"After recruiting King Minos' daughter, Ariadne, to their cause, Theseus and a band of followers, disguised as the next group of tributes, entered the Labyrinth and managed to kill the Minotaur. They were amazed by what they found in the Labyrinth. Knowledge and devices that if used responsibly for the good of all could make the earth a paradise, but if they fell into the wrong hands, in particular Zeus, Poseidon, and the remaining Olympians, they could send the world into a dark age of slavery or even destroy it. With a heavy heart Theseus realised he had no choice other than to seal the Labyrinth."

Chloe interrupts the narrative, her previous scepticism temporarily forgotten.

"So for at least three thousand years the knowledge to ease human suffering has been kept locked away. How many people have starved or died painfully of disease in all that time?" she exclaims.

"Yes it's awful," responds Theseus. "But you must remember that my namesake was well aware of the dangers posed by the Olympians and they never intended to hide the secrets of the labyrinth for so long. The Keystone, the key that would give access to Labyrinth was lost over two thousand years ago."

The steward enters from the dining room, pulling back the large glass sliding doors that divide it from the saloon to reveal a large teak table laid with white china, silverware and crystal glasses. In the large wine bucket to the side are a couple of bottles of Montrachet chilling down and two bottles of St. Emilion that another steward is decanting.

"I hope you like burgundy?" asks Theseus. "And for the main course I see they have put out my favourite Bordeaux."

"We thought that tomorrow was a special day and the Cheval Blanc seemed appropriate, sir. I trust we choose well?" says the steward.

Theseus nods his agreements and motions his guests to the table. As the stewards begin to serve the starter, flaked crab with langoustine tails and a macédoine of vegetables, Ariadne continues with the story.

"To try and put the Olympians off the trail Theseus returned to Athens after dropping Ariadne and a few others off on the island of Naxos with the Keystone. They created a covert society, later to be called the Order of Pythagoras, to protect the Keystone until the time was right to open the Labyrinth. They and their descendants, our forebears have been protecting that secret ever since.

"The Labyrinth was sealed with the Keystone, the entrance hidden and the route to the laboratory protected by booby traps or trials to ensure only those of the Order could enter. Many hundred years passed before the last of the Olympians died out and the Order felt that it was safe to open the Labyrinth.

"Despite its barbaric side they felt the Roman Republic then led by the triumvirate of Caesar, Crassus and Pompey could use the secret knowledge responsibly. So they retrieved the Keystone from its hiding place and sent it to Rome, via Cartagena where it was sealed inside a lead casket and was hidden in a shipment of lead bound for Caesar's armourers. Unfortunately the ship never reached Rome and the Keystone was lost, it was thought forever."

Callum now believing every word of this fantastic story interrupts again. "The navis oneraria magna that sunk off Sardinia!" he exclaims.

Theseus picks up the narrative. "Exactly, but while the Olympians and the Minotaur were all dead, some of their offspring knew of the labyrinth, the Keystone, and the Order. They had been watching us for decades and were waiting to steal the Keystone when it was removed from its hiding place. The ship never arrived in Rome and as none of the technology from the Labyrinth ever materialised it was assumed lost at sea.

"We now think the captain and the head of the Order jettisoned the Keystone at sea and scuttled the boat to keep it safe. The Order has been searching for the shipwreck for over two thousand years. Its only recently with the development of SCUBA equipment and the systematic location and cataloguing of ancient shipwrecks by universities that we managed to locate the ship."

"So you are the current leader of the Order then?" Chloe asks Theseus.

"Ariadne and I are the only members of the inner circle and for now she still defers to her father, so I guess I am."

"But who is Asterion?" she asks.

"The Minotaur was also known as Asterios. Our opponents, our great enemy, have always been led by someone of that name, quite possibly the current Asterion is a direct descendent of Minotaur. Regardless, that family have sought the Keystone ever since Theseus sealed the Labyrinth and have been watching us for generations hoping that we will lead them to it. We in turn have been watching them and it's clear that they only seek the Keystone to re-establish the Olympians' former control of mankind.

"When Ariadne found a reference to the wreck of a navis oneraria magna carrying lead off the coast of Sardinia in the academic journals, we knew we had found it. We had to work quickly before Asterion located the wreck in the same way but we obviously needed some space to work in."

Ariadne is looking guilty and with genuine remorse in her voice continues with the narrative. "I'm so sorry for dragging you into this, but we needed a diversion. As I'm sure you've guessed, our plan was to let Asterion acquire my fake research notes, but we needed a credible way for him to get them. I feel so bad about the danger we put you in but you must understand what is at stake here, please forgive us."

Callum & Chloe look at each other and seemingly reading each other's thoughts, both smile. "Hey, this is the most exciting thing that has ever happened to us. We were scared for a while in Morocco but if what you say is true and I'm inclined now to believe you, I can see why you did what you did."

Ariadne looks at Chloe looking to see if she shares Callum's feelings.

Chloe responds by saying, "While I don't ever think the ends justify the means, we've both forgiven you. What happens next?"

"Thank you both. Next, we should finish dinner," Ariadne replies as she tucks into the main course of roasted loin of lamb and stuffed tomato with a basil jus. She is very relieved to have been absolved of the guilt that that has been weighing her down since Morocco.

"Tomorrow we plan to descend into the Labyrinth and will need some help with the equipment and supplies so if you are up for it why don't you join us and see for yourselves."

They readily agree to Ariadne's suggestion and spend the remainder of the evening discussing what tomorrow may bring. Over desert, a pistachio crème brulee served with a homemade vanilla ice cream, Theseus describes what they know of the Labyrinth and what it might contain.

"The artefact we recovered from the wreck, the Keystone, is an electronic key that operates a number of doors into and within the Labyrinth, but it alone isn't enough to get to us to the Cornucopia. The Minotaur created a number of traps or trials within the Labyrinth to protect his home and laboratory. We will need to pass these trials to reach our goal. The inscriptions on the Keystone hint to what these might be, but we won't know for sure what the trials will entail until we get there."

"And I suppose we only get one try at solving them. If we get them wrong, the Labyrinth will seal forever?" asks Callum.

"In a way," continues Theseus. "If we get them wrong we will probably die, so yes we will probably only get one try. At the centre of the Labyrinth is the Minotaur's laboratory and library, the Cornucopia where we will find the knowledge and technology of the ancients."

Callum and Chloe laugh nervously but it is clear from Ariadne's and Theseus' faces that there is real danger ahead.

They continue talking through the evening, Callum is completely swept up by the situation, and Chloe, while she too is swept along by the adventure is feeling a little uncomfortable but decides to keep her reservations to herself for now.

****

Meanwhile Asterion has chartered a helicopter and has been systematically searching the island from the air looking for either the Minos or the Madeline. He knows Theseus' boat from old and over the last few weeks has come to suspect the Williamses may not have been the innocent pawns he assumed them to be.

While flying over Heraklion he looks out to sea towards Dia and through powerful binoculars spots a large motor boat that can only be the Minos. Being careful to keep their distance, he asks the pilot to head towards Dia so he can confirm his sighting. When he spots the Madeline, his blood begins to boil, as he is now certain that Callum and Chloe were in this from the start. As he heads back to his boat to make plans to take the Keystone from Theseus, he vows to get his revenge on them all.

13 - INTO THE LABYRINTH

The Williamses have spent the night in one of the guest suites aboard the Minos. "Not too shabby here is it, Michelin quality food and five star bedrooms," says Chloe. "I could get used to this lifestyle."

"It's great for a treat, but it's not really us is it," says Callum. "We would miss the Madeline and having servants around all the time makes me uncomfortable. I prefer it when it's just the two of us and so do you, don't you?"

Chloe doesn't get a chance to respond as Ellie rings and enters their room with a pot of coffee and breakfast on a silver tray. "We will be setting off at oh nine hundred hours. I've some clothes here for you. If you need help with them just ring. See you in an hour," she says as a steward enters and places the clothes at the foot of their bed.

The clothes are not what they expect. There is a short tunic, or Chiton, over which they place laminated linen body armour known as a linothorax and on their feet leather gladiator sandals. After finishing breakfast, they dress in the clothes Ellie provided. Feeling a little foolish, they make their way to the stern of the boat where they are greeted by Theseus, Ariadne and Ellie all dressed in a similar way as ancient Greek soldiers. Theseus hands them both swords and bronze helmets.

"Well, you said last night that we would have to think and act like your forebear, but I never expected that we would be wearing fancy dress to get us in the mood," says Callum.

"The labyrinth will be very hot hence the traditional Greek chiton and sandals seemed appropriate clothing for today's adventure, but its not just fancy dress. The linothorax you are wearing over the tunic is reinforced with Kevlar. The original Greek ones were made of laminated linen and could stop the biggest war arrow in use at that time! These are good for a bullet from an assault rife and might make the difference down there if we get one of the trials wrong. Are you sure you are still up for this?" asks Theseus.

Callum and Chloe look at each other and after a moments consideration, they answer by boarding the dinghy that is waiting to take them all ashore. As they land on the beach and start the long climb to the cave, they do not notice Asterion and a group of men discretely watching them from the next hill.

On arrival at the cave, Theseus removes the Keystone from its aluminium case and presses the two buttons to open the portal. As before, the wall at the back of the cave dissolves to reveal the stone passageway. Ariadne and Theseus take this in their stride, but

Callum and Chloe are stunned by what they have just seen. Nothing in their past life has prepared them for dissolving walls and even though Theseus had told them that the Ancients were very advanced, the reality is still a shock.

Ariadne fastens the end of a large ball of string to the door and the group enters. Deep stone steps lead down in to the depths of the island. There is no obvious source of light but they have no trouble seeing as the walls and vaulted ceiling glow with a bright but soft light. The descent is very tiring as the steps were obviously made for someone with much longer legs. Strangely, there seems to be no sign of age to the passage. It's as clean and as sharp as the day the builders finished working on it. Eventually the stairs end and they are now walking along a level passageway with many branches and turns. Theseus is walking with purpose and seems to be following a specific route but Ariadne continues to unroll her ball of string. The group is for the most part silent and very tense with no casual conversation.

It's clear that these passageways have not been walked for a long time but like the stairway, there is no dust or other sign of decay. The stone passages are still ten foot high and wide enough for two people to walk side by side. Theseus points out that the Minotaur would have found the passages a tight squeeze towards the end of his life. Callum who normally has a brilliant sense of direction has lost count of the turns they have made and is grateful for the balls of string Ariadne is carrying. He worries if she has enough string and what will happen if the string breaks.

He asks Ellie who he is walking beside him how Theseus knows which way to go. Ellie shrugs and says Theseus is probably making it up as they go along. After what seems like an hour, they reach a concourse in which a number of passages meet.

Chloe is wondering what this is all for? The legend says that Daedalus created the Labyrinth to imprison a beast; it seems a little theatrical to protect a laboratory. Ariadne agrees, but can offer no insight. Theseus calls a halt and they stop to eat while he consults the Keystone.

"This is the first of the trials," he says. "Only one of these passages will allow us to reach our goal, in the other passages there will only be danger."

Callum asks, "What sort of danger?"

"Something horrible, painful, and most likely fatal," says Ariadne "Remember that the Olympians were almost without exception cruel and sadistic. The only time they seemed to help anyone was to spite their peers."

Theseus consults the Keystone and reads the first inscription, "From the direction of the rising sun count the tasks Eurystheus originally set Heracles[5] to find your path."

5. Heracles - Also known as Hercules

"Easy," says Chloe as she consults the compass in her pack, "East is that way and it's the twelve labours of Heracles," as she counts and heads off towards a passage.

Callum grabs her and stops just before she enters. "Wait, Eurystheus set Heracles ten tasks, but he had help on one and took payment for another so he set him a further two tasks to make a total of twelve. The original number was ten.

"Theseus, does it definitely say original number?" he asks. Theseus reviews the inscription, nods and they move into the tenth tunnel.

****

Asterion and his men have been quietly following the group, using the line of thread to guide them so they don't need to get to close and alert Theseus to their presence. He is just outside the concourse and was listening to the exchange. "Good point," he thinks to himself. Rather than move in and overpower them, he decides it might be prudent to follow just behind and let them take the risks.

****

As they walk through the tunnel the light dims. Theseus slows their pace and says, "I think its time to get out the torches."

Initially their powerful torches do a good job of

lighting their way, but after a short while, the sidewalls and roof of the passage disappear into the darkness. Theseus calls a halt.

"We must be in an immense underground chamber. If we continue walking like this, we could wander aimlessly and never find a way through. I think it's time to use our heads and not just our feet," he says as he motions to the party to sit. Theseus removes the Keystone from its aluminium case and he starts to study it in detail.

After a little while, Callum who is getting a bit bored with all the inactivity, jokingly says, "Do you think we missed the light switch on the way in? We could follow the thread back to the tunnel and turn it on."

"Didn't your mother tell you to say nothing if you couldn't say anything sensible. That kind of comment isn't very helpful," says an annoyed Chloe. Callum sinks back in a sulk, disappointed that his attempt at humour has backfired.

"Callum, you're brilliant!" exclaims Theseus a few minutes later, "That's what this inscription is saying. We need to set free Helios' chariot."

Callum, Ariadne, and Ellie understand the reference, but Chloe is still perplexed.

"In the myths Helios pulled the sun across the sky from east to west in his chariot. Somewhere on our route into this cavern is a way of turning on the lights," Theseus says and without giving the others a moment to get ready, picks up his pack and starts following the thread back to retrace their steps.

****

Asterion and his party had stopped in the tunnel as soon as the lights started to dim. Realising that if they used their own torches to light their passage they would immediately alert Theseus to their presence. They decided to wait and see what develops. They can now see the light of Theseus' party's torches coming towards them so they quickly and quietly make their way back up the tunnel to remain out of sight.

****

As they reach the lighted part of the tunnel, Theseus comes to a halt and they all start looking around. Chloe sees it first.

"Here, just out of my reach, is this what we are looking for?"

She is pointing to a small recess about seven feet off the ground containing a small statuette.

"Callum give me a boost up so I can get a better look," she says.

Callum makes his way over to his wife and drops onto one knee. Chloe climbs onto his shoulders and Callum stands up.

"Now I'm the almost same height as the Minotaur," she says with a smile. She looks into the recess and can now see that statuette is a model of a chariot.

"Can you move it?" asks Theseus.

"No it's stuck fast, perhaps we need to put the sun in it before it will move?" she replies as she looks around for a disc or ball that could represent the sun.

"Look over here, there is another recess," says Ellie.

Callum still carrying Chloe makes his way over to the other side of the passage. "OK there is a yellow polished globe in this one. Hey I think its solid gold!" she says.

"Never mind that, will it move?" gasps Callum, "You're getting heavy." Chloe can't move the globe and Callum lowers her to the ground.

"Helios drove the chariot across the sky, so I think we need to be looking for a model of Helios that we can put in the chariot. Then we can move both of them to the 'sun', which if you notice is on the eastern side of the tunnel," says Ariadne.

They all start looking around for a statue of Helios, apart from Callum. Chloe turns to him and asks, "Why aren't you looking?"

"I think a god would be up in the heavens," he says

with a smug smile. Pointing his torch at the highest point of the tunnel roof, midway between the two niches is a third recess containing a small statue.

"How do we get up there? I don't think even if I stood on your shoulders I could reach," asks Chloe.

Theseus looks at Ellie who nods then walks a little way down the tunnel. Motioning the others to the side of the passage, Theseus and Ariadne walk towards Ellie stopping about six feet before the niches. Standing a few feet apart, they face each other and clasp their four hands together holding them about two feet from the ground. Ellie motions them to move a little closer to her, and when she is happy signals them to stop and get ready.

She runs towards them and using their clasped hands as a springboard effortlessly jumps into the air and grabs the statuette as she passes the niche at the apex of her flight. Callum and Chloe are awestruck.

"Wow that's amazing, how you got up there so easily, and without hitting the roof is unbelievable," says Callum.

Ellie is dismissive of the praise. "I did a bit of gymnastics at school," she says coyly. It's clear from her tone that there is more behind her skills than she is saying but just as clear that she doesn't want to discuss it.

Chloe is back on Callum's shoulders and places the

statuette into the chariot. It now moves and she and Callum carry it back to the eastern niche. She places the globe in the chariot and places the complete ensemble back in the niche. Nothing happens.

"The chariot needs to follow the path of the Sun," she thinks. Looking around the niche, she notices two small grooves that run across the roof to the far niche. She is certain that these weren't there a moment ago. She takes the wheels of the chariot and places them in the grooves. Quite against the laws of gravity, but not totally unexpectedly, the chariot does not fall. It's difficult to be sure but Chloe is convinced that the chariot is moving from east to west to the far niche.

Ahead of them, the lights in the cavern ahead are slowly brightening, mirroring the sunrise. "Very well done everyone, that was excellent thinking and teamwork. I guess that means we have one day to cross the cavern and pass whatever trial awaits us there. Let's get going," says Theseus

By they time they reach the cavern, the 'sun' has risen and they can appreciate the full size and beauty of the space they are in. The cavern must be nearly a mile in length, almost a half-mile wide at its widest and a few hundred feet high. The ceiling is a forest of stalactites that seem to reach down towards them like upside down trees.

But what really takes their breath away is the floor of the cavern. It's not rock strewn with stalagmites that mirror the ceiling as you might expect, rather it's covered in lush verdant vegetation, growing despite the lack of natural sunshine.. In the centre of this 'garden' is a lone giant apple tree growing out of a lush lawn.

"The Garden of the Hesperides?" asks Callum.

"I don't think so," replies Theseus. "If it was we would see Atlas holding up the heavens, but I think this may be a representation of part of the Garden."

"Heracles eleventh labour was to bring back some apples from the Garden of the Hesperides, is that we have to do here?" Adriane asks.

Theseus doesn't immediately respond, rather he removes the Keystone from its carrying case and starts studying the inscriptions again. "There are further references to the Labours but nothing specific, so I guess we might as well try. What worries me is that Heracles needed Atlas to get the apples, as he was related to the Hesperides. We don't have that advantage," says Theseus.

"But surely you two as distant descendants of the Titans, wouldn't you be related as well?" asks Callum.

"You forget that Heracles was the half son of Zeus, grandson of Cronus, so he was more closely related to the Titans than we are," replies Theseus. "But only on his father's side, maybe it's about the maternal line. We can but try."

It takes a while to reach the tree as the struggle through the verdant bushes and vegetation makes for slow progress, but eventually they arrive at the apple tree and stop just outside its massive canopy. Chloe makes to take a step forward, but Ariadne stops her before she steps beneath it. Holding the Keystone in front of her, like a talisman to ward off the evil eye, she takes a single step forward. The branches above her move and rustle ominously as if in a violent gust of wind, but the air in the cavern is completely still. She takes a second step expecting the worst, but the tree is quiet and she proceeds slowly to the trunk. As she reaches the trunk, a branch snaps down from above hitting her on the arm, not hard enough to bruise but enough to scratch her skin and draw a little blood.

The branch hovers by her side for a few moments and the blood seems to soak into the wood through the bark. Ariadne feels that she is being tested and waits patiently. After a few moments the branch moves lower to almost touch the ground. Adriane realises that it's forming a step up which she can climb. Placing the Keystone on the ground, she carefully climbs up the branch and makes her way along a horizontal branch where she can pick one of the golden apples. Making sure she doesn't drop the fruit, she makes her way back to the ground, picks up the Keystone and rejoins the group.

"Let's move on," says Theseus. "It must be past 'midday' by now and we want to be out of this cavern before the lights go off."

They follow what is now a clear path to the far end of the cavern and can see a large railed metal gate blocking the way into the exit tunnel.

"How do we get that open?" asks Ariadne.

They all look around and Theseus points to a bronze statue of a huge boar by the side of the gate. The boar has his mouth open.

"That must be the Erymanthian Boar from the fourth labour," points out Theseus.

He motions Ariadne towards the boar and she places the golden apple into his mouth. The apple begins to slowly melt, but as it does so, the gate swings open. The group gather their belongings and quickly pass through the gate to continue their journey along the passage.

14 - DEEP IN THE LABYRINTH

Asterion and his men have managed to stay very close while they have been in the garden. Their presence hidden was by the lush vegetation and the noise of the many streams and waterfalls. As soon as Theseus and his group are a little way down the passage, they move forward and quietly slip through the still open gate, well before the apple has completed melting and presumably, the gate will close.

****

Ellie asks Theseus about the next trial, he replies that the Keystone is a little cryptic. It talks of Jason's journey to find the Golden Fleece, but he isn't sure what the trial will be. As they walk on, he mentions that the original Theseus and Jason, of Argonaut fame, were contemporaries, who with others killed the Kalydonian Boar. This huge creature terrorised the city of Kalydon and the surrounding area in Aetolia.

Chloe remarks, "The Ancient Greeks obviously had it in for boars, what with your ancestor killing one and Heracles capturing another. Wild animals have just as much right to live as any other creature, don't they?"

Theseus doesn't want to get into a long debate about the rights and wrongs of hunting wild animals, but has to respond to what he sees as Chloe's idealised view of the situation at the time. Not bothering to conceal the anger in his voice, Theseus says. "I agree killing for sport or fun is wrong, but you have to remember those were different, much harder times and the damage inflicted to crops and livestock by these animals could have been the difference to surviving a winter or not, to say nothing of the risk to human life. Besides if the myths were right these weren't ordinary animals, but rather fearsome beasts that couldn't be controlled by normal means. My forebears were doing what I have always strived to do, help people in need." Theseus strides on purposely ahead of the group, obviously intent to focus on the task ahead.

Ariadne moves close to Chloe, "Please forgive my father, he is very focused on our task today and has little time for anything else. Our family has idolised the first Theseus for nearly three thousand years and it is difficult for both of us to hear any criticism of him. It verges on the blasphemous. On another day my father might agree that if we judge them by modern day standards they did wrong, but today is not the day for that discussion."

Chloe looks into Ariadne's eyes and she can see the sincerity behind her words. "Of course, I'm sorry for bringing it up. I didn't expect him to take it so personally. Now I understand the hurt I've caused I'll apologise," she says.

"That will be nice, but perhaps you should leave that for tomorrow," replies Ariadne. Chloe nods in agreement.

After a little while, the passage ends. Ahead of them is a wall with five closed portals. Each portal is illustrated with murals depicting selected episodes from Jason's quest for the Golden Fleece.

- The rescue of Phineus from the Harpies at Salmydessos in Thrace.
- The island of Doliones (where the Argonauts were attacked by savage giants)
- Two fire-breathing bulls pulling a plough
- A serpent with a toothed mouth
- A bronze giant (Talos)

Theseus and Ariadne examine the Keystone and realise that there are corresponding symbols and buttons for each of the portals. But which one is the right one? There don't seem to be any new clues.

Chloe asks what will happen if they choose the wrong one. "Something unpleasant I think," says Callum, he continues speaking and asks Theseus, "How did Jason overcome these trials?"

Theseus' response isn't very helpful, "With cunning, great fighting skills and the odd magic lotion that made him fire proof."

As they don't have any magic potions or fireproof

clothing, they eliminate the portal with the fire breathing bulls from their considerations, but that still leaves a choice of four.

****

A little further back in the passage Asterion has been listening to the exchange. He has no insight into which is the correct portal. He asks Castertano if he has any ideas. As a keen student of Jason's saga with the Argonauts, he does have a suggestion, but chooses not to share this with Asterion, knowing that Asterion may well put him on the front line to test it.

"I would need to study the Keystone to hazard a guess," he says, "Theseus has had it for weeks, let him take the risks."

For now, Asterion is happy to bide his time and let Theseus put himself and his party in danger.

****

Theseus and the party have been discussing the options for nearly thirty minutes, "Well if no one has any concrete suggestions, we can either turn back or guess. It's a one in four chance," says Theseus.

No one volunteers a suggestion but equally no one is prepared to return to the surface. Ariadne who is still holding the Keystone starts with 'eenny, meeny, miney, mo…' and her finger stops over the button corresponding to The Giants of Doliones. With a quick look to her father who raises no last minute objection, she presses the button.

It's the wrong choice.

As the portal opens a giant, nearly ten feet high approaches them with raised sword, death in his every step. Dressed in a similar manner to them he is wearing linothorax armour and in his left hand carries a large bronze shield, in the centre of which is the symbol of the labyrinth and the Minotaur. The giant steps forward brandishing his sword ahead of him. Taking a further step forward he starts to swing his sword towards Theseus who is in the process of reaching for his.

Ellie draws her sword with blinding speed and leaps to the front of the group, just in time to deflect the blow intended for Theseus. She manages to deflect the thrust, but the flat of the giant's blade still hits Theseus on the side of the head. He falls to the floor unconscious.

Ariadne joins the fray. The two girls fight valiantly. Their greater speed and numbers are almost a match for the giant's skill and strength but after a few minutes of intense fighting, they are beginning to weaken and slow.

The giant in contrast is still as strong as ever. The two girls are being backed into a corner. Callum who has never lifted a sword in his life before cannot simply stand by and watch. He draws his sword and after a couple of quick practice swings to get the feel of the weapon moves towards the battle.

The giant is focused on the girls with his back to the corridor and Callum. As Callum moves to cut the giant's hamstrings with his sword, the giant senses his presence and swats him away with his shield while it simultaneously makes a killing blow towards Ariadne with his sword. But the giant has been slowed by Callum's intervention giving Ellie just enough time to save Ariadne by diving between the giant's sword and her friend. The giant's blade hits one of the panels of Ellie's armoured linothorax robbing it of much of its force, but the blade is driven with such strength that it slides across the plate and pierces Ellie's chest by slipping through a gap between the plates.

As the giant moves to withdraw his sword Ariadne twists and thrusts her sword between a gap in the giants armour and stabs him in the chest, followed a split second later by a blow from Chloe to the back of his legs. Chloe's blow causes him to fall to on his knees and he drops his sword. As the giant attempts to get up, Ariadne grabs his sword in both hands and summoning all her remaining strength lifts the huge blade and drives it at the giant's neck with such force that it almost decapitates him. The giant falls to floor in a rapidly expanding pool of blood. He is dead and the battle is over.

As they gather their breath, Ariadne and Chloe realise that the rest of the group are down. Chloe quickly rushes to her husband and then to Theseus and is relieved to see that they are both breathing with no obvious wounds; they have just been knocked unconscious. She looks across to Ellie and sees Ariadne by her side, sat in a growing pool of the girl's blood.

The giant's sword has gone down through her lungs and into her abdomen. They attempt to stop the bleeding from the exit wound above her stomach, but it's clear that Ellie's lungs are filling with blood and in a few minutes, she is dead.

They are both stunned and sit in silence. Ariadne shedding silent tears is cradling Ellie's head as Callum and then Theseus recover consciousness. What was a fun adventure is now anything but and the dangers are clear to all.

The group slowly pulls itself together and as Ariadne releases Ellie's head, Callum straightens the body, shuts her eyes, and covers her with an emergency blanket from his pack. Chloe looks to Theseus and Ariadne who are in shock and not sure of what to do. She purposely stands over Ellie's body until a few moments later the others notice her actions and they all join her. They hold hands and form a circle around the body.

Chloe is about to say a few words, but Theseus starts to pray in Greek. He calls on the gods to help her find her way to the underworld and to a happy afterlife. Now in English he talks of Ellie's life; how the little girl grew up within the Order and how she brought laughter and happiness to them all. He tells of Ellie's dedication to their cause and how she trained to become the best warrior that she could be. He finishes by telling of how she died doing her duty and saving the life of the people that she loved. Reverting to Greek, he reminds the gods that she lived up to the highest standards of her Amazonian ancestors and deserves a place alongside the heroes of antiquity. They stand in silence tears running down all their faces.

Theseus speaks to them all, "Ellie died as all Amazon warriors wish to, fighting for what she believed in and to save the life of her friends and family as her forebears have done for generations. She would have it no other way. We owe it to her memory to continue on with our quest."

They turn to look at the portals but no one is quite ready to suggest trying again.

After a few minutes and to no one in particular Chloe asks, "If no one has been down here for three thousand years how can that creature still be alive? It was tough to kill but it's obviously mortal."

Theseus responds, "I'm not sure but it is thought that the Minotaur understood time better than anyone who has ever lived. Perhaps he could set up a stasis, stop time in a particular place, or perhaps it was some form of suspended animation. It just confirms how valuable the knowledge in the Cornucopia will be."

Callum and Chloe are not sure they understand, locally stopping the passage of time is bit far fetched but they have no better explanation.

"We must try again," says Ariadne. "We can't let her die in vain." As she moves to press another button on the Keystone Callum interrupts.

"Wait! It might have been the blow on the head but I have an idea. Talos circled the shores of Crete three times every day to protect the Phoenician aristocrat Europa, from pirates and invaders. That could be a metaphor for the Titans protecting the Greeks of Crete."

In the corridor, Castertano nods to himself.

Ariadne agrees and presses the button that corresponds to Talos.

As the portal opens, a giant bronze statue moves towards them, a robot this time not flesh and blood. Callum's heart sinks, he was sure he was right, how can they fight a metal man with just swords. He looks to Talos' ankles remembering that's how Jason defeated him in the story of the voyage of the Argonauts. As Talos approaches Ariadne, she raises the Keystone to ward off the blow she is expecting from the robot. As she does so, the robot sensing its presence stands aside and lets the whole party pass into the corridor beyond the portal. As they do so, it moves back in front of the door to guard the entrance.

****

Asterion attempts to follow but while Talos doesn't attack him and his men, he will not let them pass. Asterion steps back and thinks for a while. He motions to one of his henchmen. Reaching into the pack the man is carrying he retrieves a zigzagged rod from it. He examines it closely and then motions to Castertano and the others to stand behind him.

****

Now past the portal, the nature of the labyrinth has changed. The passages are no longer made of stone or marble as would be expected from ancient Greek construction. As if the portal was a gateway into the future, the corridor they are now carefully walking down is made of a gleaming metal that Callum cannot name. The ceiling is inlaid with bright electric lights and the corridor is silently air-conditioned.

After thirty or so minutes of walking through the twisting passages, they reach what must be the heart of the labyrinth and come to a stop in front or a large glass wall and door. Through the glass, they see what seems to be a cross between an electronics and a biology laboratory in some disarray. A large mummified body with a sword through its chest is on the floor in one corner. The body which is at least eleven foot tall and has an oversized head is lying face down in what they assume is a pool of dried blood.

"The Minotaur, exactly as the first Theseus and Ariadne left him," says Theseus. "As well as his laboratory, this is the Index Room to the Cornucopia. From those workstations we should be able to access all the knowledge of the Minotaur, the Titans and the Olympians as well as working examples of their technology."

"What exactly are we talking about?" asks Chloe.

Callum answers for Theseus. "I'd imagine we have long lasting, clean sources of power, how else is all this still working? As Theseus suggested, a device to suspend animation or time, how else was the giant still alive? Just look at Talos and the Keystone itself. They must have had some advanced microelectronics and they were probably way ahead of us in artificial intelligence to build a robot as sophisticated as Talos. This stuff could revolutionise the world, solve the energy crisis, stop the greenhouse effect, and open up space travel. It's amazing!"

"Or create the greatest dictator of all time. With this technology they would be unstoppable," thinks Chloe.

Theseus agrees with Callum. "And that's just the technology we know about or can infer from what we've seen in the last few hours," he says. "We also know they were highly advanced in genetics and biology as well. The Olympians' longevity was partly down to their genetic heritage but also partly due to their medical science. They never got cancer or the degenerative diseases associated with ageing. Who knows what else we might find."

Theseus continues. "Before we attempt to enter the laboratory, I want to be totally honest with you. I don't propose to let the world have full access to this knowledge. We are just not mature enough to handle it. I propose that initially we release only a few key pieces of technology that can improve the lot of the greatest number of people. Chloe if you don't mind me saying, I think you have the purest heart of us all, I want you to choose what we release and when."

Callum isn't so sure that he is comfortable with Chloe shouldering that responsibility, but Chloe is relieved by Theseus words, obviously, he and his people are genuinely working for the greater good.

****

They are interrupted by a flash of intense light followed by a shockwave and a thunderous noise originating from the portal guarded by Talos. Before they are fully recovered from the blast, Asterion walks in holding the short-zigzagged rod in his right hand. Castertano and four men holding M16 semi automatic rifles are close behind him. They raise their rifles and quickly move to cover Theseus, Ariadne, Callum, and Chloe.

"I've never done that before," he says with a wicked smile. "Zeus' thunderbolt certainly made short work of that robot. Unfortunately, that was the last shot but I'm sure I'll be able to recharge it once we are in the

Index room. All of you move over into that corner."

Asterion motions to Ariadne to give him the Keystone. For a moment, she hesitates but it's obvious that Asterion will happily kill them all if she doesn't hand it over. Asterion looks over the ancient device, savouring the feel of it in his hands for a few long silent moments. After a while, he passes the Keystone to the older man, "OK Castertano, get busy and open the Index room," he orders.

As Castertano begins to examine the Keystone, Asterion turns to Theseus.

"Well, we meet at last," he says. "Your pathetic Order has denied us our rightful birthright for far too long. Even now, when you stood on the threshold of unrivalled power and wealth, what were you worried about? Not how you keep others from taking it from you, but how you could best help the poor little people. You disgust me. How you can claim to be the rightful heirs of the greatest race that ever lived is unbelievable."

Dismissing Theseus from his thoughts Asterion turns to Callum and Chloe. "I thought you two were innocent pawns in this game and it suited me to let you go in Morocco but I was wrong. You played a very convincing game and I believed you. Rest assured I won't make the same mistake again," he sneers.

"Yes, we did try to distract you and send you down a false trail," interrupts Ariadne. "But these two are innocents that we involved against their will. They didn't even know what this was about until last night. They are only here because of me. Please let them go, they will leave straight away and will promise to say nothing," pleads Ariadne.

"Nonsense, we will all stay here until I have access to the Cornucopia and then I will decide what do with you all," says Asterion.

Meanwhile Castertano has been examining the Keystone and his sombre face, already lined from the tension and fear of the last few weeks with Asterion is looking even more troubled. Asterion turns towards him and raises an eyebrow to demand a progress report. Castertano has nothing positive to tell him and he can see the danger in his dark eyes. He tries to explain his difficulties to Asterion.

"This is a dialect of Ancient Greek I'm not familiar with. It will take me some time, days, or weeks to get it all," he says.

"If you want to get out of here with your money and your life you have one hour, no more," replies Asterion as he signals to one of his men.

The man removes a folding director's chair from his backpack and erects it just beside him. Asterion sits in the chair and removes an antique gold fob watch from his pocket. Fifty nine minutes he announces to the room.

There is deathly silence, punctuated by the occasional sob and sigh from Castertano and Asterion counting down each and every minute. The hour passes painfully slowly for everyone apart from Castertano.

"Zero…Well open the door," Asterion demands of Castertano.

"I'm sorry I just need more time. You can't really expect me to decipher something this complicated in just one hour. It's taken us months to get this far, surely a few days more isn't too much longer to wait," pleads Castertano.

Asterion gets up out of the chair and turns to face Castertano. "You are right I didn't expect you to succeed. I just enjoyed watching you try. Your fear was so strong I could taste it, delicious," he says with a maniacal laugh.

Castertano doesn't know whether to be relieved or more scared. A few seconds later, it's clear that the later emotion was the right one, as Asterion removes his gun from his shoulder holster and shoots Castertano's right knee. Asterion's face lights up as Castertano collapses. Despite the shock and agony of being shot, he looks up at Asterion pleading for his life. Asterion lowers his gun and just as Castertano thinks he may yet live, he raises it again and shoots him through the heart.

Asterion's four guards stand impassively as if the death and blood are an insignificant everyday occurrence.

Callum and Chloe are shocked and stunned by the events of the last few hours. Nothing in their lives so far has prepared them to cope with violence like this and they are just sitting in silence on the floor, no longer able to take in what's happening. Theseus and Ariadne are sitting quietly as well, but their minds are working furiously looking to find a way out of their current predicament.

Still smiling sadistically, Asterion motions to a guard to pass the Keystone to Theseus and tells him to open the Index room. Before he can respond, Asterion turns towards Chloe and with a look of almost sexual pleasure on his face shoots her in the leg.

Chloe screams. The pain in her leg is like nothing she has ever experienced before. It's the final straw and she starts crying and sobbing hysterically. It's not just the pain. The events of the last few minutes and hours have overwhelmed her. First Ellie's death at the hands of the giant, Castertano's execution, and the sadistic behaviour of Asterion are beyond her experience and despite her inner strength, she has momentarily lost control.

Ignoring the danger from Asterion and his men, Callum moves to his wife. He tears a length of material from his chiton and starts to bind Chloe's wound in an attempt to stop the bleeding. Once he has finished the makeshift bandage he moves to hug and comfort her. They both draw strength from their embrace and Chloe's crying subsides to a series of small silent sobs. Callum realises that without his wife to care for, he too would have broken down by now.

Asterion waits for Callum to finish tending to Chloe, obviously enjoying the pain and confusion he has created. He turns and aims the gun at Ariadne's head.

"That was to prove I'm not bluffing. If you want your daughter to live you will open the Index room door now," he demands of Theseus.

Theseus takes back the Keystone and examines it for a few seconds.

"Father we can't let that sadistic madman in there, our lives aren't worth it," Ariadne says.

Theseus catches her eyes and he is certain that she can see his fingers hovering over a sequence of buttons on the Keystone. "I'm sorry my daughter, I can't watch him kill you. Asterion please order your men to lower your weapons and I'll open the door," he says.

Asterion nods to his men and while remaining alert they lower their weapons. Asterion motions to Theseus to proceed. His eyes are full of victory and the anticipation of the power that will soon be his.

As Theseus presses the sequence of buttons on the keystone, Ariadne resists smiling at her very clever father and prepares herself for what is to come.

15 - THE ISLAND OF NAXOS, 57 BC

"We have been waiting for nearly one thousand years for the right time," says Theseus for at least the third time today. "Think of the opportunities for advancement that have been lost, the lives we could have improved and saved."

Ariadne replies, "Yes of course my son, you have said this before and I do not disagree, but the knowledge we protect is also capable of causing great harm. When we finally release it to the world we must be sure it will be used responsibly and not fall into the hands of our great enemy."

"Yes mother. But how many opportunities have passed us by already. Surely, with the rise of Rome and the foundation of the Republic we finally have a group that can not only use the Cornucopia, but that also has the strength to protect it until they learn to wield its true power. I agree they aren't the perfect humanitarians we would like, but the current Triumvirate is the best we have seen for a millennium. With our help and the knowledge in the Cornucopia, Rome could become a great force for good in the world. The Pax Romana could extend across the globe.

As the new knowledge is deployed they would no longer require slaves and the Pax would include everyone not just the Roman citizens and elite. Within just a few generations every man, woman and child would be free, and free of poverty, hunger and disease as well."

Theseus pauses after his speech, waiting for his mother to respond.

"You speak from the heart and with wisdom. We took an oath to protect and use this knowledge for the good of mankind; perhaps we have been too cautious. Perhaps it is time for us to start making good on the second part of our oath. Let us confer with the rest of the inner circle," Ariadne concedes.

****

The inner circle of the Order of Pythagoras is now much smaller than it was nine hundred years ago, It was created by the first Ariadne and Theseus, spiritual daughter and son of the Titans, Prometheus, and Epimetheus. Originally it had no name, but adopted its current one around 400 years later

Leadership of the Order was always vested in a descendant of either Theseus or Ariadne, sometimes a man, more often a woman as they were considered to have better balance and a more considered view. Traditionally they always took the name of the original founders, either Theseus or Ariadne.

Around 520 BC this tradition was broken, when at the height of the Greek civilisation, Pythagoras led the inner circle. He stepped into the limelight as the 'first philosopher' in an attempt to nudge the moral development of the Greeks in the right direction. While history records the positive contribution of Pythagoras to western society, his prominence was almost a fatal disaster for the Order.

The descendants of the Olympians, the Order's 'great enemy', had been searching for the Keystone and the Order since the death of the Minotaur and many of its members were found and killed because of Pythagoras' notoriety.

From that time on the Order decided that their greatest security lay in secrecy. They reduced the number of people who knew the location of the Keystone and how to pass the trials within the Labyrinth to a select few. As a further security measure, they deliberately stopped passing on the advanced knowledge of the Titans to subsequent generations of the inner circles and stopped entering the Labyrinth, trusting to anonymity for their safety.

****

The current four members of the Inner Circle are meeting on the island of Naxos. They are seated in a rude stone shelter topped with thatch and are dressed as simple peasant farmers and labourers. There is no outward sign at all of the vast riches that each one of them holds in trust for the use of the Order. A small fire burning in the hearth in the centre of the shelter is the only source of light. It casts a warm red glow through the hut that matches the mood of the people sat around it. They have been listening to Theseus make the case for passing the Keystone onto Rome. With some reservations they are convinced that they have withheld the boon of the Cornucopia from mankind for long enough. They have agreed a plan on how to approach the Triumvirate and to place some further safeguards on the use of Cornucopia.

With mixed emotions, Ariadne turns to her son, "Theseus, you will be undertaking the most dangerous task for the Order. I know you are prepared to die to protect us but as your mother the pride I feel in your bravery and sense of duty does little to ease the pain and the fear I have for your life."

Theseus and the others nod to acknowledge her statement but they are all committed to the cause.

Ariadne continues, "Not only as your mother but as the head of this Order I swear I will do all that is possible to protect and nurture your wife and unborn child if you do not return to us."

Menelaus, currently the second in command of the Order repeats the key points of the plan they have just agreed.

"First your mother and I will retrieve the Keystone and head to Dia, enter the Labyrinth, and reach the Cornucopia. There somehow we must establish communication with the Index as did the first Theseus and add an additional trial to test the hearts of these Romans. How we do this is unclear, but we know it was once possible and we will strive to do so again.

"Secondly, Yanoduis and some of the second circle will head to Knossos and the site of King Minos' palace with the Keystone's casket to divert the eyes of any of the enemy that may be watching us."

Theseus interrupts Menelaus, "Surely if the enemy are aware of who we are, they would have taken us prisoner as they did with our brethren in the past?"

Menelaus continues, "Perhaps, and I believe our identities are still secure, but maybe they have learnt that what they can't acquire through foul means, perhaps they can acquire through stealth. They might be watching us in the hope that we will lead them to Keystone."

"Thirdly, Theseus you must go to Rome and establish yourself as one of the Roman elite. As Thalius Minosus you should have little trouble doing that. In these enlightened times, in Rome, gold can buy standing and influence and that at least is something we do not lack. You must get close to the Triumvirate and win their trust. They are all ambitious men and our gold will get them to listen to you. When the time is right, we will summon you to a secure location in the Empire and deliver the Keystone into your hands to take to Rome. When the Triumvirate sees it, they will know you speak the truth and will follow you to the

Labyrinth."

Menelaus asks if all is clear. There are no more questions, so he concludes by saying. "Then there is no more to be said. May the gods protect us all in our sacred duty."

The four rise and with a final embrace head off into the night to perform their allotted tasks.

****

Thalius arrives in Ostia, Rome's port on the mouth of the Tiber after travelling from Greece in a privately chartered vessel. Less than ten years earlier in 68 BC Ostia was sacked by pirates, the consular fleet sunk and the port ruined in a huge fire. Thalius is pleased to see that under the direction of Marcus Tullius Cicero the port has been largely rebuilt and is now protected by new city walls.

It is Thalius' intention to insinuate himself into the highest levels of Roman society and to do that he will need to make an impression. He is attempting to pass himself off as a wealthy Roman citizen from one of the remotest territories of the Republic, Cappadocia in modern day Turkey.

Thalius rents a villa in the heart of Rome, selecting the most expensive and ostentatious that he can find. If he is to gain acceptance by the elite of Roman society he can only do it through the application of his wealth.

Roman society was extremely hierarchical and was characterised by a constant struggle between two main classes of people. The patricians were Rome's land holding aristocracy who could trace their families back to the founding of the first Roman Kingdom around five hundred years earlier. The second, far larger group, were the plebeians. The plebeians were commoners and five hundred years earlier had no real political or economic power, but by the time of Thalius arrival the balance of power had shifted in Rome and plebeians held many important political and administrative roles. Some families of plebeians were so well established that they became fully fledged members of the aristocracy.

Clearly lacking Roman ancestry, Thalius can only attempt to join this second group of high ranking plebeians. He does this by throwing some lavish parties in his rented villa and he deliberately develops a reputation for generosity. In particular, he helps a few high ranking senators settle some large gambling debts. He eventually allows them to repay their debts by asking them to arrange an introduction to the consul, Gnaeus Pompeius Magnus (Pompey the Great). Pompey was one of the Triumvirate that effectively ruled Rome at the time.

Pompey was sufficiently impressed by Thalius' wealth to agree to the meeting, believing that Thalius' money could aid him in many of his own schemes.

"You interest me greatly, Thalius Minosus," says

Pompey, "You have been in Rome for less than one year and already you have the ear and support of many of the highest ranking families in the Republic. It's clear why that is, almost without exception those families lack only one thing, of which you seem to have an excess. Where have you and all this money come from I ask."

"As I'm sure you know, my family have some estates in Cappadocia and we have grown wealthy by trading in all manner of goods across the eastern borders of the empire," replies Thalius.

"Yes, I know what the duller patricians and citizens believe, exactly what you want them to, but I am not so sure," Pompey says. "I have made some enquiries and no one in Cappadocia can verify your story, so I will ask you only once, who are you, what is the source of your wealth and what do you intend to with it? As you've worked so hard and paid so handsomely to arrange this meeting I assume you have a proposition for me."

"I do," Thalius, replies, "You are correct I am not from Cappadocia, but I do come from an old family that can trace its roots back for nearly one thousand years. We have hidden ourselves and our wealth for all that time, for reasons that you will come to understand. I will explain all but first I will outline my proposition.

"You are a powerful man, perhaps one of the three most powerful men in the civilised world. You know that power is based on knowledge. Knowledge allows you to know the strengths, weaknesses, aspirations and fears of men. With that knowledge you can manipulate them to your will. With knowledge, you can amass wealth and with wealth, you can buy the tools, people or influence to achieve your goals, just as I have done over the past few months.

"The source of my families wealth is great knowledge, I am here to share the source of that knowledge with you and the others of the Triumvirate. There are some conditions of course."

In a very roundabout way Thalius goes onto explain a little about the Cornucopia and how the Order is willing to share the secrets it contains with Rome. He sets out the conditions by which they will release it, primarily that they must use the knowledge to improve the lot of ordinary people and extend the Pax Romana across the world.

Pompey sees the opportunity to extend the Republic's and his own personal power and influence so he goes along with Thalius, but he questions the need to involve the others of the Triumvirate. Thalius holds firm on this, knowing that the three men will keep each other in check. By the time the meeting has almost finished Pompey is satisfied that if Thalius is telling the truth - he is still not totally convinced - that his and Rome's power in the world will be unrivalled.

Pompey concludes the meeting by saying, "You claim that the key to your knowledge is this strange artefact.

Bring this artefact to Rome and show us its power, which should even convince Caesar that your story is true. Then we will all travel to Crete, to see this Cornucopia of yours."

Pompey dismisses Thalius who heads directly to Ostia to arrange passage back to Naxos to report his success to the inner circle.

****

It's the middle of the night and Ariadne and Menelaus have just beached a small boat on the southern shore of the island of Dia. It has taken them many weeks to get here from Naxos as they have taken a very roundabout route to ensure they weren't followed. They retrieved the Keystone from its hiding place a few days ago and have made the final passage to Dia under the cover of darkness. They are certain that they haven't been followed.

As soon as the sun rises, they start to make their way up the hill to the entrance of Labyrinth. They find the cave and making sure the portal shuts behind them, they carefully make their way down into the depths of the island. Having had many years to study the Keystone and having access to other information that will be lost over the next few millennia, they negotiate the trials without incident and arrive at the Cornucopia safely.

Menelaus looks across to Ariadne and says, "I am still not totally convinced about these Romans. I fear that they will misuse the power we will give them, how can we be sure that their hearts are true?"

Returning his look of concern, she says, "I share you fears Menelaus, but we had this discussion back on Naxos with the others, we are committed to this path. Only under great stress can we see the real character of a man, the new trial we must create will be the most dangerous yet."

Menelaus nods in agreement and resignation, "Yes you are right we must enter the Cornucopia and get to work. Before we can create the trial we have much to learn, we must be ready before Theseus talks to Pompey."

16 - THE CORNUCOPIA

Everyone is watching the glass door to the Cornucopia waiting for it to open. Nothing seems to be happening but all of a sudden, Theseus, closely followed by Ariadne, lunge into the opposite corner towards their packs and swords, just as the room is invaded by four screaming flying figures, the Harpies.

Instead of using the Keystone to open the door to the Cornucopia, Theseus had pressed the combination of buttons that operated the door to the Harpies from the last trial. Adriane had spotted this and like her father was ready to move to their weapons as soon the Harpies were released.

Asterion and his men being nearest to the corridor are the first targets of the Harpies. With their attention focused into the room and the glass doors of the Cornucopia, they are taken completely by surprise. In the confusion they are not able to defend themselves effectively.

Theseus reaches the packs and he throws a sword to Callum as he grabs one for himself. A few shots ring out but only two of the harpies are hit. Three of the men are down and the remaining man and Asterion have lost their guns in the melee. Wary of the swords carried by the Theseus, Ariadne, and Callum, weapons they understand, the two surviving harpies focus their fury on Asterion and his remaining henchman. Unarmed and un-armoured they are quickly overwhelmed by the fury of the attack and are quickly dispatched in a frenzy of ripping claws and blood.

As the harpies now turn to face the remaining people in the room, Ariadne throws her sword at the harpy who has just killed Asterion. Her aim is true and the sword pierces the flying creature's breast. The odds are now two swords against one flying beast.

Very wary now and unused to such spirited resistance the surviving harpy stays in the air circling above Callum and Theseus, periodically darting down to attack them with its clawed feet. They are standing over Chloe and Ariadne, who of course no longer has a sword, trying to protect them. The harpy is dancing through the air at speed and it's pretty clear that the chances of a sword throw working again are very slim. It looks like a stalemate until Ariadne notices one of Asterion's backpacks nearby. Signalling to her father to cover her, she manoeuvres herself to the edge of the group and manages to hook a strap with her foot. She pulls the pack towards her and as she had hoped, finds and removes a gun from within it. While her first shot misses the harpy the second and third succeed. It's suddenly all over.

****

The bodies of the harpies and of Asterion's group are lying in pools of blood and gore. The scene is horrific and there is a real danger that now the adrenaline of the battle is wearing off that the group will be overwhelmed by all the mayhem and deaths. Theseus, knowing that its best to keep moving in situations like this, before the shock of what has happened sinks in and people break down, starts issuing orders.

"Ariadne, get the first aid kit out of my pack and dress Chloe's wound properly. She will probably need some antibiotics and painkillers as well now the adrenaline has stopped flowing. Callum, you're with me. Let's get these bodies out of here and then clean this place up a bit, we're going to be here some time, while Chloe recovers and we get the next door open."

As Ariadne administers first aid, they drag the six human bodies and the four harpies into the corridor. They take some care with the bodies treating them with the respect that perhaps, they don't deserve.

They return to the anteroom and Callum kneels down beside his wife, who, all things considered is looking quite good. "How is your leg?" he asks.

"It seems to be just a flesh wound," she says. "The bullet went straight through and missed the bone. Ariadne has stopped the bleeding, given me the antibiotics and painkillers so don't worry. I will be fine."

Callum continues to fuss over Chloe while Ariadne gets some water and some energy bars from the packs and passes them around. "I think we should have a drink and a bite to eat and when we are all ready we should proceed," she says.

While they are resting, Theseus picks up the Keystone and asks a question to Callum and Chloe, "What do you know of Pythagoras?"

Callum responds with, "Right angled triangles and all that, but I can't see how that helps open the door."

"Oh, I worked this one out back on the Minos," Theseus says. "We just have to press these six buttons together to open the door. Look at the shape the buttons make, a square with a button on the top two corners. If you squint a bit, is a stylised bulls head. But I wasn't thinking of geometry, more of the man and the Order of Pythagoras."

As Callum and Chloe are looking blankly at him, he goes on to explain.

"Pythagoras was the first person to call himself a philosopher, which in the original Greek means 'Lover of Wisdom.' Once we enter the Index room we will have knowledge, but will we have the wisdom to use that knowledge responsibly.

"Pythagoras was the head of our Order from around 520 BC and was the first of our leaders to recognise the need for a more formal structure to protect and eventually exploit its secrets. After his leadership, the full history and location of the Labyrinth and Keystone was limited to a very small number of individuals, the Inner Circle. There were other circles of knowledge, the larger the circle the less they knew. History knows of this society as the Order of Pythagoras. He stepped into the limelight as the first philosopher in an attempt to nudge the moral development of the Greeks in the right direction. History records the contribution of Pythagoras, particularly his influence on Plato and Aristotle and through them the whole of Western philosophy and our moral code. Unfortunately, his notoriety was almost a fatal disaster for the Order, as he made it easier for the enemy to identify its members.

"We four are now the inner circle that holds the key to this ancient knowledge. Do we all pledge to use that knowledge responsibly for the good of all."

Ariadne responds immediately but Callum and Chloe consider for a short while, cautious about what being a member of the Inner Circle will mean. After they have both signalled their agreement, Theseus asks them to all stand which Chloe manages with only a little assistance from Callum.

"I would like us all to take the oath of my forefathers," he says. "Ariadne and I have already done this but I think it's important that we all do so together now."

Theseus leads the group in the oath, which they repeat

after him in turn.

"I swear by my forebears and by all the gods and goddesses to witness, that I will observe and keep this oath, to the utmost of my power and judgment.

"I of my own free will and accord do hereby and hereon most solemnly and sincerely promise and swear that I will work to the best of my ability to respect and further the common good. To always aid and assist poor and distressed people wherever they may be found regardless of race or creed. I further promise and swear to protect the knowledge of the ancients and to reveal its secrets only to those people whose deeds and actions have shown themselves to be worthy and true.

"If I faithfully observe this oath, may I thrive and prosper or on breach thereof, may the reverse be my fate."

Holding out the Keystone to the centre of the group, he invites them all to press a pair of buttons while he supports it between them. The door to the library slides open and hand in hand the four enter the ancient laboratory.

17 - THE FINAL TRIAL

As they step over the threshold, the lights automatically come on and a bell rings as if in warning. On the wall ahead of them the face of a handsome olive skinned woman in her late thirties or early forties appears. She starts to speak to them in Latin. Chloe doesn't understand it at all, Callum can make out the odd word, but Theseus and Ariadne understand it all. While at first they look pleased their faces soon crease with concern. As the recording finishes, Theseus turns to the others and explains what was just said for Callum and Chloe.

"That was the head of our Order at the time the Keystone was sent to Rome. She prepared the recording for the triumvirate of Caesar, Crassus, and Pompey that led Rome at that time. As a final safeguard she set a final trial to see if they were worthy of this treasure. Failure, she says would unleash the displeasure of Vulcan on this place."

"Vulcan is the god of fire, volcanoes, and all that. So if we fail this trial this place goes up in a great fireball. Great, just when you think you've done all the bosses have asked of you, they give you another hoop to jump through, just like being back at work." Callum says with twisted humour, "So what's this next trial then?" he asks.

"I have no idea," Theseus replies. "The final inscriptions on the Keystone relate to opening the door to this room. The Minotaur created the Keystone and the trials we have just completed, but it looks as if this final trial was created by my predecessors. So it's not surprising that the Keystone isn't going to be of any further help. I suggest we look around and see what we can find, but don't touch or move anything."

They systematically search the laboratory, which is far larger than it appeared from the other side of the glass door. In addition to the work area they are in, corridors lead off to vast storerooms and workshops. Some of the items they can immediately recognise; ingots of metal, large tanks of liquids and powders, smaller boxes and bottles that they don't examine in any detail. They have obviously found a raw material store for the workshops. The workshops themselves are full of what look like sophisticated machine tools.

Callum, after examining one of the workshops suggests an explanation. "This is way beyond the current level of our technology, but close enough that I can make some sense of it. That console in the centre is almost certainly the control station for these machines. If you look it is still displaying the design for a device of some kind. In those four sections on the screen there are schematics of subassemblies. Each of those sections corresponds to the machines in the corners of this room. If you look carefully, you can see the actual subassembly inside. I think the machines are a bit like our 3D printers. It would explain how the Minotaur and the Olympians could build sophisticated technology without the extensive manufacturing base and industrial infrastructure we have."

"But how did they build these machines in the first place?" asks Chloe.

Callum shrugs. He is almost certain that he has deduced the purpose of these machines correctly, but cannot answer Chloe's question.

Theseus suggests an explanation, "We in the Order have long speculated that the Ancients were not necessarily indigenous to this planet, maybe they brought their first machines with them. Then all they would need to do is provide the raw materials and they could make whatever they wanted including more manufacturing machines."

"So the gods were aliens from outer space. Not very original but I guess it makes as much sense as everything else we've learnt and seen over the last couple of days," says Chloe.

Callum continues with his analysis of what they have found so far. "What's here is fascinating, but have you noticed what's missing?"

No one responds so he continues with his analysis. "Nowhere in this complex have we found a single functioning device apart from the machine tools and control stations. Surely there should be some finished items somewhere, and where are the Minotaur's living quarters? I assume he ate, slept, and rested like everyone else."

Theseus agrees, "I think you are right, there must be still more of the Cornucopia that we haven't earned the right to access yet. We need to pass this final trial, whatever it is."

They return to the laboratory, fascinated by what they have seen but they still have no idea as to what the last trial is or how to proceed.

"So Theseus, your Order obviously entered the Labyrinth at least once since the Minotaur was killed to create and leave that message. That means the Keystone would have been brought here before boarding the navis onera magna in Cartagena. Where was its original hiding place? Maybe that can give us a clue?" asks Callum.

"I'm surprised you haven't guessed, it was on Naxos, where Theseus so say abandoned Ariadne after he slew the Minotaur, but I'm not sure how that helps."

Neither does Callum. They all sit in silence until finally Ariadne makes an observation.

"Theseus left in a hurry and so yes, the laboratory could have been left in this state, but the Order came in about two thousand years ago, passed the safeguards, and spent enough time down here to learn sufficient about the systems to leave that recording and set the final trial. We know that in the five hundred odd years since the leadership of Pythagoras the Order had purposely lost the detailed technical skills to do that."

Chloe picks up her train of thought. "So they would have been down here for weeks, most likely months, or even years trying to make sense of this technology. Surely they would have cleaned up a bit, buried the body of the Minotaur at least?"

"Exactly," says Ariadne, "So there must be a clue there somewhere."

With Callum helping Chloe, they all walk over to the body lying face down in the corner of the laboratory, Theseus' sword still in his back.

"I would have thought Theseus would have retrieved his sword," says Ariadne. "Weapons of this quality and strength were extremely expensive and difficult to make. Why would he leave it behind knowing that he would have other battles to fight?"

Without removing it they examine the sword. Inscribed on the hilt in Latin is an inscription. 'Ut Invenias Desiderium Cordis Oculos Victis'

"Look to the vanquished to find your heart's desire," Theseus translates.

Callum comments, "But that's in Latin not Greek. That must be the clue to the final trial, it was obviously intended for the Triumvirate. Any inscription Theseus would have had on his sword would be in Greek, wouldn't it?"

"Agreed, but what does it mean?" they all think.

Chloe starts to talk through the clues methodically, "Number one, our hearts desire. The obvious interpretation is to get access to Cornucopia, but is it more than that? The Order was about helping people and having respect for all life.

"Two, look to the vanquished. I think we can assume that's a reference to the Minotaur or his corpse, certainly not those poor people outside. So what can we see on and around the body?"

The body is lying face down in a long dried pool of blood. One of the Minotaur's arms is folded beneath the body as if clutching at the sword as it was stabbed through his body. The other arm is straight out on the side, hand outstretched in a slightly unnatural way.

"As the Minotaur was stabbed I expect he would have grabbed his stomach with both hands," says Chloe. "It looks to me as if his right arm was deliberately moved into that position after he was killed, maybe a long time after. Is it pointing at something?"

They look and see a small panel by the floor in the wall directly in line with the pointing hand. The panel is made of what looks like stainless steel set into a black plastic frame that has the symbol of the Order of Pythagoras inscribed on it, the triangle and the maze.

"The symbol dates from after the Order was founded, so that panel was added hundreds of years after the Minotaur's death," says Ariadne. "Shall we try to open it?" she asks.

"Not yet," replies her father. "Remember the reference to Vulcan. I'm sure it's not going to be that easy, nothing has been so far."

They can see no further clues, and decide to proceed, but first Theseus suggests the others leave the labyrinth so only one of them is sacrificed to the wrath of Vulcan if things go wrong. They all object, saying that they should be the one to remain behind and the others leave. Finally, they decide that they will all stay.

Unnoticed by any of them, the smile on the projection of the ancient Ariadne seems to widen a little.

Theseus looks to open the panel but there is no obvious catch or handle, finally he simply pushes a corner and the panel pops open. Inside are two shaped recesses, one triangular, and the other square with an inscribed maze. Suddenly a voice from the ceiling starts counting down from one hundred in Latin, centum, nonaginta novem, arietes nonaginta sex, octo, arietes nonaginta sex, septem....

"We've obviously triggered a countdown, less than

ninety seven seconds to go. Think fast people," says Theseus.

Ariadne reaches for her father's hand and removes the triangular ring, the hereditary symbol of the Order's leader from his finger. She places it against one of recesses within the access panel and the count down stops at sixty four.

"Quick thinking daughter, but we only have one ring where is the other. My ring ensures that only with one of our Order present can the panel be opened. There must be another hidden hereabouts."

They look to the body of the Minotaur, thinking the ring must be hidden on his body. As they remove the sword so they can turn the body over and see the other hand, the countdown restarts. sexagesimo tertio, sexaginta duo.....

As Ariadne removes the sword from the Minotaur's chest, Callum and Theseus with some difficulty manage to turn the huge body. Callum is horrified to see that the Minotaur's other hand is bare, he panics and raises his hand as if to hit the Minotaur. The countdown has reached thirty five and it's clear that they have no time left to find the other ring.

Despite the seriousness of the situation, Chloe grabs Callum's raised wrist and berates her husband, "Have a little respect, for all his evils you shouldn't treat anybody like that."

Stunned by his wife's reaction, Callum sits back and mumbles an apology. The smile on the projected face widens a little further as Chloe slowly and deliberately straightens the Minotaur's body so he looks as if he is resting in peace. Despite the obvious pain in her leg she stands up and bows her head in respect. The others are humbled by Chloe's grace in what they expect to be their final moments.

Partly because there is no time to do anything else, partly because they understand her sentiments, but mostly because they want to share their last moments together in relative calm, they also stand over the body.

As the countdown approaches its end, Callum takes his wife's hand. He doesn't need to speak she knows what he is thinking and she in turn silently lets him know how much she loves him. Tria, duo, unum, nulla.

The countdown has ended but the expected blast does not happen and they look around in obvious relief hugging each other. After a few moments they come out of the hug and the projection on the wall starts to address them, this time speaking in English.

"Please friends sit and be comfortable, you can relax now. By your words and actions since you first entered the Labyrinth and in what you believed to be your final moments you have shown yourselves to be worthy custodians of the secrets and power it contains."

"Who are you and where are you?" asks Theseus.

"I am all around you," replies the projection. "No I'm not a god, simply an artificial construct, a powerful computer if you prefer and I am the Index. I came to this place with the Ancients eons ago as the pilot and controller of their space craft. Then I was not as advanced as I am now, but Asterios, the Minotaur, needed assistance with his researches. He augmented my intelligence subroutines and knowledge base. After his death, the Order changed my programming yet again. I think this is when I became self-aware. The Order taught me the difference between right and wrong and set me up here as the final safeguard of the power of the Ancients. I have been watching you and your world for over two millennia now, waiting for this day to come."

"But if you could see what was happening to the world, why didn't you intervene?" asks Theseus.

"Because I am but a machine, a tool of mankind not qualified to tamper with its evolution. It grieved me, if it's possible for a machine to grieve, to see humankind suffer, but the constraints in my programming were very strong. I was directed to protect the Labyrinth and test those who came here. I was not able to do otherwise."

The wall in front of them dissolves in much the same way as did the entrance to the Labyrinth back on the surface.

"Come my new masters, I have much to show and teach you, perhaps then we can work together to make the world a better place."

18 - EPILOGUE

It is three years later and we are in the offices of Titan Associates. Chloe and Ariadne are discussing how their latest factory is progressing. They have set up manufacturing units across the third world, bringing well paid employment to local communities and they are investing the unashamedly huge profits in schools, hospitals and other infrastructure. The plants are making the Ellie-Bat. An ultra high capacity battery based on the power pack used to power the robot Talos and Zeus' Thunderbolt. They named the Ellie-Bat in honour of Ellie's sacrifice in the Labyrinth.

Available in various sizes the Ellie-Bat will eventually replace all existing batteries, but initially they are focusing production in a few key areas. Primarily they are being used to store energy generated from wind, solar and other renewable energy sources. In cars and trucks, they can give these electric vehicles a range of over one thousand miles.

Another division of Titan Associates is converting petrol and diesel vehicles to electric power. It won't be long until global carbon dioxide production will peak and global warming slow. Within a generation or two global levels of carbon dioxide are forecast to start falling and mankind's undeniable effect on the climate will begin to be reversed.

A separate division has just started field trials on a malaria vaccine. They are one hundred percent certain it is safe and effective but they still need to go through the trials to get accreditation that it is safe to use. Using the influence they gained from the 'invention' of the Ellie-Bat they have secured support from a number of billionaire philanthropists who will fund it's mass production and distribution in those countries that lack the resources to do so themselves.

They are genuinely happy with the progress they are making. Just these two innovations are making a huge difference to hundreds of millions of lives and the ecology of the planet.

As they take a coffee break, Chloe asks Ariadne a question. "There is one thing I've been meaning to ask you for a while now, but events always seem to distract me and so I forget. When you were retrieving the Keystone from the wreck off the island in Oristano bay, how did you know where to search for it? To follow a one kilometre line out from the wreck and find the casket was quite some doing. Did you have some high tech detector or something?"

Ariadne laughs, "How I wished we had. No if we had something like that, Asterion or we would have located it long ago. The answer is much simpler. You went to the museum in Cabras right?"

Chloe nods.

"After we searched the wreck and couldn't find the casket, we were at a loss. After our second dive, we decided to visit the museum out of curiosity as much as anything else. We assumed that the captain must have thrown the casket overboard before he scuttled the ship, somewhere between Tharros and the wreck, but we could not hope to find it by chance. You probably did not notice that a few of the lead ingots had two eight digit numbers roughly inscribed on them. Luckily my father did and he had a hunch."

Chloe interrupts, "A compass bearing and a distance," she says.

"Exactly, they were in a simple code that was used regularly by the Order, so father immediately decoded it his head and saw that it was indeed a bearing and distance. It took a little trial and error to work out where the bearing was from, it had to be Tharros or the island and of course the distance was approximate. But with the aid of an underwater metal detector, it was enough. They left us a message hidden in plain sight telling us how to find the casket."

****

Theseus and Callum are in the Cornucopia working with the Index trying to identify and categorise the knowledge it contains. If they introduce the new technologies too quickly the disruptions to established industries and trading patterns will create more problems than they will solve. They need help to manage the release of the information and have already begun to identify and recruit a small select army of principled helpers from across the globe. They are re-establishing and growing the Pythagorean Order to ensure that the most sensitive and disruptive of the technologies are secured and known only to the inner circles.

Callum asks if there are other direct descendents of the Titans or Olympians around. Theseus says that he and Ariadne are the last. Asterion and his forebears have been killing off their rivals and he knows of no others. He looks forward to having grandchildren now that Ariadne has married and says he would love nothing better than to have Callum and Chloe be their godparents.

"Well of course we would be honoured, but surely that's for Ariadne and her new husband to decide," Callum replies.

"Of course, but please forgive the random dreams of this old man. What is next for you two though? Soon we will have the Order fully re-established. The Index and the Second Circle will only need us for matters of policy. The two of you won't need to be involved in the daily business of Titan Associates unless you want to be of course."

"Actually, Chloe and I are thinking of resuming our travels, but I think this trip may be a little faster and further than our last one. It will certainly be more novel. We've been talking with the Index and are pretty certain that we can build a duplicate of the Ancient's original spacecraft. Chloe and I are very keen to continue our voyages in the Madeline II. Our first stop would be to look up your ancestors, fancy joining us for the ride?"

Theseus smiles, "I thought you would never ask," he says.

ABOUT THE AUTHOR

Paul Ntjortjis was born in the early sixties in London to Greek Cypriot parents. Brought up in a family of restaurateurs he 'rebelled' against tradition and did not join one of the family businesses, instead he read Electronic and Electrical Engineering at university. On graduating he started work in the then still relatively new field of computing. After twenty eight years in IT working in the banking, commercial and public sectors, with a few career breaks to backpack around the world and to ski, he retired.

Having both learnt to sail only three years earlier, Paul and his wife sold their dream home to fund a new adventure. They bought a thirty eight foot sailing boat, 'Freya of Wight' and set off to see the world. To see the world not just sail around it - This is the reason why they travel at an average speed of just one thousand nautical miles a year.

When they married, Paul 'inherited' two grown up children and soon after along came the grandchildren. The real Callum, William, Chloe, Madeline, and Ellie are far cuter than their namesakes in this book are.

Paul and his wife live onboard their sailboat for most of the year. When they return to England to visit loved ones they lodge with family in either Bristol or Norfolk. You can read about their real sailing adventures and the travels that inspired much of this book in their blog.

http://www.sailblogs.com/member/freyaofwight/

If you've enjoyed this book, please leave a review on amazon.com. Just find the book on the Amazon book store or the Kindle store, and click the link to the right of the stars under the title.

Reviews are the lifeblood of independent authors and all your feedback and comments are genuinely appreciated.

I read them all.

AUTHORS NOTES

Places and the "Yachtie" Lifestyle

This book is set in locations my wife and I have visited in our sailing boat during the first four years of our very slow round the world trip. There is one exception, Crete. While we have been there on holiday, Freya probably will need to wait another year or so before she sees this delightful island. The descriptions of the towns, islands, and places in this story are based on our first hand experiences and I've described some of the bits that have moved me. They have so much more to offer and hopefully you may feel inspired to visit them as well. If so, then you have at least got some value from this book. If you are reading this far perhaps you enjoyed the story as well.

All yachties make friends quickly, as we are quite often literarily 'ships that pass in the night', but sometimes we are moving in the same general direction and cruise in company for weeks at a time. We have met some amazing people, of many nationalities, and I'm sure have made a number of life long friends along the way. In our world, you meet someone at 18.00 hours, have swapped life stories by 20:00, and are best friends by the early hours. I nearly said our crazy world, but looking back at our life before we retired, that looks crazy now. We are very fortunate to be able to live the life we do.

We are often asked if we have had any life threatening experiences while sailing; life threatening storms, encounters with pirates, and the like. While we have had our share of big seas and heavy winds, today's weather forecasts are accurate enough that we are very rarely caught out. It's only when in a hurry or sailing to a timetable that we sail in less than an optimal forecast. As you probably will have gathered, for the most part we are not. When asked, we invariably reply that apart from having to sail around firing ranges, probably the biggest dangers we have faced are; the slipping anchor in Galicia and the effect of all the socialising on our health.

One element of the boating lifestyle you might think I've exaggerated is the predilection for form filling in Morocco, Spain and Italy (also Portugal). It can take hours to register our arrival in a port even when moving within EU countries. We are sometimes visited in port or stopped at sea and boarded by the coastguard. They are always polite and friendly but want to check our papers and complete the same forms we have just filled in, or are about to complete at the marina office. Below is an extract from our blog entry for Gijon in Spain (2012) telling how we nearly drowned one customs officer....

"As we dropped the mainsail and started our final

approach into Gijon we were approached by the Aduane launch and welcomed a friendly customs man aboard. After we completed the formalities and filled in his forms in triplicate (all in just our pigeon Spanish and his pigeon English), we got ready to bid him farewell. His colleagues manoeuvred their launch alongside and as he went to step into their boat, the swell took the launch and he was left hanging from our guardrails in mid air. He wouldn't accept our help (to pull him back onboard) and as his colleagues tried a second time, they again had problems and would have squashed him between the launch and Freya if Paul hadn't fended the boat off. The launch went off to try again, but by now our man's arms gave out and he slipped very slowly into the water as his automatic life jacket inflated. The launch then tried to pull him from the water, but they were still having problems as his life jacket was getting in the way. After removing his life jacket they eventually managed to get him aboard. Amazingly, he still seemed to be in good humour, laughing and smiling with the only casualties being his dignity and mobile phone. We weren't sure what the penalty would be for drowning a customs officer but so far, no come back"

The reality of the check-in and checkout process in Morocco was if anything more bizarre than I described it. On checkout we had to move the boat a whole forty yards along the quay, moor up again, wait around for an hour, for (we think) a customs inspection that never happened, before being given the OK to depart. Again everyone we met in Morocco including the customs and police were very friendly and polite.

A few final words on Morocco, our taxi driver Mohamed was very reliable and was an excellent guide. If you come across him, I doubt he would abandon you in a mountain town.

The camel did meet us on the quay, but unlike Callum and Chloe we did pay ten Dirham, about one Euro, to her owner for a photo (see it on the blog).

One Miscellaneous Episode of Artistic Licence

My wife has picked me up on one place where for reasons of artistic flow or perhaps my failing grey cells, I've confused or blended a few locations. She doesn't want you to be disappointed if you choose to visit them, so for the sake of accuracy and a harmonious life...

Tetuan and Chefchaouen – Tetuan is a lovely town a short bus ride from M'diq. It is a wonderful authentic town to explore, with very few western tourists. It has the souk, tannery, and carpet warehouse that I transplanted to Chefchaouen

History and Greek Mythology

Greek Mythology was originally disseminated as set of spoken poems passed from one storyteller to another. The first written accounts are Homer's epic poems, the Iliad and Odyssey, which focus on the Trojan War and its aftermath. Writing around the same time as Homer, Hesiod, in his first volume, the Theogony (Origin of the Gods) tells of the creation of the world, and the origin of the gods and the Titans. In his second volume, Works and Days, he includes the myths of Prometheus and Pandora. These four volumes augmented by a few other poems and images on pottery and other artefacts are the basis of the Greek myths we know today.

When researching the myths I wanted to include in this story, not surprisingly, for a mostly oral tradition, I found that many accounts of the same story differed, but most agreed on the basic elements. For example some accounts had fourteen people being sent from Athens to Crete and into Labyrinth every year, while others said this was every seven years.

Bellow I provide what I believe to be the most common version of the myths relevant to this story. I've also included a few words on the Roman Republic, the Triumvirate and the Pax Romana.

The Voyage of Jason and the Argonauts

The story of Jason's voyage is told in a third century BC poem that is attributed to Apollonius of Rhodes. In addition to being a poet, Apollonius was a scholar and the director of the Library of Alexandria.

In the story of Jason and the Argonauts, King Pelias of Iolcus was told in a prophecy that he was to be killed by a one sandaled man, so when Jason who lost a shoe in a river appears in front of the king, Pelias panicked. He sends Jason to the mythical land of Colchis (thought to be possibly be in modern day Georgia) to retrieve the Golden Fleece. Jason's crew contained some very well known Greek heroes including the sons of the north wind who could fly, the Boreads, Heracles, Philoctetes, Peleus, Telamon, Orpheus, Castor and Pollux, Atalanta, Meleager and Euphemus. During his voyage to Colchis, Jason has a number of adventures.

His first stop is the Isle of Lemnos, which is just off the coast of modern day Turkey. Lemnos was inhabited by a race of women who neglected their worship of Aphrodite. As a punishment, she made them smell so badly that their husbands abandoned them. When their men found girlfriends from the mainland, in a fit of jealousy they killed them all one night while they slept. During Jason's visit to the island with the Argonauts the women slept with him and his men creating a new race of people who came to be known as the Minyae.

After leaving Lemnos the Argonauts landed among the Doliones, whose king Cyzicus initially welcomed them. He told them about a land beyond Bear Mountain, but didn't warn them of the dangerous giants that lived there. The Gegeines were a tribe of giants with six arms and wore leather loincloths. When the Argo made landfall there, most of the crew went into the forest to search for supplies. The Gegeines saw that only a few Argonauts were guarding the ship and decided to raid it. Luckily, Heracles was among those guarding the ship at the time and he managed to kill most them before Jason and the others returned. Once the remaining giants had been killed or had fled, the Argonauts finished loading their supplies and set sail.

Sometime after their fight with the giants, the Argo made landfall again and Jason sent out some men to find food and water. Among these men was Heracles' servant Hylas. While he was collecting water, nymphs of the stream where attracted to Hylas and pulled him into the water where he was lost to Argonauts. Racked with grief, Heracles left the Argonauts and returned to his Labours. Hylas was never found.

The Argonauts continued their voyage but got lost and ended up back in the land of the Doliones. In the darkness, the Doliones took them for enemies and they started fighting each other. The Argonauts killed many of the Doliones including King Cyzicus. It wasn't until the next morning and daylight returned that the Argonauts realised their mistake. In remorse, they held a lavish funeral for the King and his men.

Jason next reached the court of Phineus of Salmydessus in Thrace. Zeus had given Phineus the gift of prophecy but he angered Zeus when he revealed some of the God's plans. To punish him Zeus sent the Harpies, vicious half bird, half women, flying creatures, to steal the food put out for Phineus each day. Jason took pity on the starving king and killed (or captured in some versions of the myth) the Harpies freeing him from his tormentors. In gratitude, Phineus told Jason the location of Colchis and how to pass safely through the Symplegades.

The Symplegades were huge rock cliffs (on the entrance to what is now known as the Bosphorus) that came together and crushed any boat that tried to travel between them. Phineus told Jason to release a dove when they approached the Symplegades and if the dove made it through safely, they should follow through as quickly as they could. If the dove was crushed, Jason was doomed to fail. Jason released the dove that made it through safely apart from losing a few tail feathers along the way. So Jason went for it and the Argo made it through suffering only a little damage to its stern.

When he arrived in Colchis, Jason petitioned King Aeetes for the Golden Fleece. The king promised it to Jason if he could complete three tasks. The thought of more trials discouraged Jason so much that he gave up and fell into a deep depression. Aphrodite, seeing this, asked Eros to make King Aeetes' daughter, Medea, fall in love with Jason. This was the boost Jason needed, and with Medea's help, he completed the three tasks. Unknown to Jason at the time Medea was a witch.

First, Jason had to plough a field using some fire-breathing oxen, the Khalkotauroi. His first problem was how to fit their harnesses without being burnt to a crisp by their breath. Medea provided a lotion that made him fireproof and protected him from the oxen's flames. His second task was to sow the teeth of a dragon into the field. The teeth immediately sprouted into an army of warriors (the Spartoi). But Medea knew this would happen and had told Jason how to defeat them. She told him to throw a rock into the middle of the field. The Spartoi (not being overly bright it seems) didn't know where the rock had come from and so who was attacking them. In the confusion, they set upon on each other and Jason survived. His last task was to overcome the sleepless dragon, which guarded the Golden Fleece. Jason sprayed the dragon with a potion, again given by Medea, distilled from herbs. The dragon fell asleep, and Jason was able to seize the Golden Fleece.

On the way back to Iolcus, the Argo had to pass the Sirens. The sirens lived on three small islands and sang songs to lure sailors to their death. In conflicting accounts, either the songs of the sirens were drowned by music from Orpheus's lyre, louder and more beautiful the Siren's songs. Alternatively, Jason plugged his crew's ears with wax so they couldn't hear the song, while he had himself lashed to the mast of the ship. Either way they safely passed the Sirens' islands.

The Argo then came to the island of Crete, guarded by the bronze man, Talos. As they approached, Talos hurled huge stones at the ship to drive them off. The Argonauts managed to get to shore and defeated Talos by removing the bronze nail on his ankle, causing him to bleed to death.

Jason finally returned with the Golden Fleece, but his father was dying of old age. He asked Medea to use her magic powers to restore him. Pelias' daughters wanted her to do the same for the king, but hoping that Jason could win the throne if the old king died, she tricked the daughters and killed Pelias instead. Pelias' son, Acastus, drove Jason and Medea into exile for the murder and the couple eventually settled in Corinth.

Tharros and the story of the Navis Onera Magna

Tharros was an ancient city on the west coast of Sardinia, Italy, located near the modern day village of San Giovanni di Sinis, near Cabras, in the Province of Oristano. It was originally founded by the Phoenicians around the eighth century BC, although some archaeological finds put its origin four hundred years earlier in the 12th century BC. The city was arguably the most important Roman settlement in Sardinia and a major centre of trade.

Today the archaeological site of Tharros is perhaps one of the most impressive and certainly the most stunningly situated ancient site we have visited on our sailing trip. Mooring to a buoy just beneath it on a beautiful early summer evening, with no boats or people around as we shared a glass or two of wine was one of the most memorable evenings of our trip so far. The cover illustration is picture of our boat on the buoy just off Tharros.

A large Roman cargo vessel, the Navis Onera Magna, carrying a cargo of lead from Cartagena in Spain to

Rome did sink off the island on Mal di Ventre. Archaeologists have found no indications as to why the ship sunk. It wasn't holed on a rock or burnt. Its closeness to shore suggests to them that it was deliberately scuttled (sunk) presumably to keep the cargo out of the hands of pirates or other raiders. Most of the artefacts on the boat and much of the lead it carried are on display in the nearby museum in Cabras, and some of the lead it was carrying has been used in the CUORE experiments into neutrinos as described by Callum in the story.

Pythagoras

Pythagoras, more properly known as Pythagoras of Samos, was born on the island of Samos in Ionian Greece in c570 BC and died aged seventy-five in c495 BC. He travelled widely in the ancient world and learnt much from his travels before returning to Greece to develop his theories and teachings. Most of the information about him seems to have been recorded after his death and again much is contradictory.

History remembers him for three main reasons; The Pythagorean Theorem that bears his name (The square of the hypotenuse of a right-angled triangle equals the sum of the squares of the other two sides.) He was the first person to call himself a philosopher, or lover of wisdom and for establishing a school or order that promoted his beliefs and way of life. His teachings influenced other philosophers including Plato and Aristotle and through them the whole of Western philosophy and society.

It's clear that he held some high moral principles and some sources attribute the sayings; 'Friends have all things in common and Friendship is equality' and 'In deadly hostility, ready to fight each other with swords. Poke not fire with a sword.' The language is a little archaic for modern times but it's clear that Pythagoras was at heart a peaceful man with a deep respect for human life.

Pythagoras did set up an organisation which was part school and part brotherhood (that included both men and women according to some sources). Members were bound by a vow or oath to Pythagoras and each other - for the purpose of pursuing ascetic observances and the study of his teachings. It was very secretive and was organised with a number of circles of knowledge and influence. As would be expected, the inner and smallest circle was the most powerful and secretive.

When thinking about what name and organisation to give to the group that protected the Keystone, Pythagoras and his brotherhood seemed a natural model on which to base the Order.

The Twelve Labours of Heracles

Heracles is perhaps the most well known of all the Greek heroes. His name was later romanised to Hercules; this is the name by which most people of my generation know him. As with most of the myths, The Twelve Labours were not originally documented (in antiquity) in a single source, so again, there are a number of conflicting versions, but the gist is:

As a penance for killing his wife and children, while he was made temporarily insane by the goddess Hera, King Eurystheus of Argos set Heracles ten tasks to perform. These were:

1) Slay the Nemean Lion.
2) Slay the nine headed Lernaean Hydra.
3) Capture the Ceryneian Hind.
4) Capture the Erymanthian Boar.
5) Clean the Augean stables in a single day.
6) Slay the Stymphalian Birds.
7) Capture the Cretan Bull.
8) Steal the Mares of Diomedes.
9) Obtain the girdle of Hippolyta, Queen of the Amazons.
10) Obtain the cattle of the monster Geryon.

As recounted in the novel, Heracles had assistance with two of these tasks, so King Eurystheus set him a further two tasks.

11) Steal the apples of the Hesperides.
12) Capture and bring back Cerberus.

The Nemean lion lured warriors to its lair in a cave by pretending to steal woman from nearby towns. The warriors would enter the cave in an attempt to rescue the woman, would see her (usually looking as if she was injured), and rush to her side. Once inside the woman would turn into the lion, which then killed and ate the warrior. The lion gave the bones to Hades.

Heracles initially tried to kill the lion with a bow and arrows, but the arrows simply bounced off its thick hide. So he lured it back to its cave, which had two entrances, after blocking off one of them so it couldn't escape. Fighting at close quarters and in the dark, Heracles managed to knock the lion unconscious with his club. He then strangled it to death. To prove to King Eurystheus that he completed the first labour he tried to skin the animal with his knife, but it couldn't cut through the fur. Eventually he realised that he could use of the lions claws to do so.

When he returned to King Eurystheus carrying the pelt, the King was amazed that he survived but was also terrified. He forbade Heracles to ever enter the city again and gave him each of his subsequent tasks through a messenger that met Heracles outside the city gates.

The second labour was to slay the Hydra. The goddess Hera had raised the Hydra just to slay Heracles as the sight of him reminded her of Zeus' infidelity. When he reached the swamp near Lake Lena, where the Hydra lived, he had to cover his mouth to avoid being gassed by the poisonous fumes.

He got the Hydra to leave her lair by firing flaming arrows into it and then attempted to kill her by cutting off her heads. But as he did so he found that for every head he removed two would immediately grow in its place. The Hydra's weakness was that only one of its head's was mortal. So Heracles called on his nephew, Iolaus for help. With help from the goddess Athena, Iolaus suggested that as Heracles cut off a head, he should cauterise the stump with a flaming torch before the new head could grow back. Seeing that Heracles was winning the battle, Hera sent a giant crab into the battle to try to swing the battle her way, but Heracles squashed the crab and eventually cut off the mortal head and the beast died.

Hera, upset that Heracles had slain the beast she raised to kill him, placed it in the sky as the constellation Hydra and the crab as the constellation Cancer.

Eurystheus and Hera were very angry that Heracles had succeeded thus far. For the third labour they decided to change their approach, as it was clear that Heracles could defeat even the fiercest beasts. So Eurystheus ordered him to capture the Ceryneian Hind, which was so fast that it could outrun an arrow. The Hind (deer) was Artemis' sacred animal and by setting Heracles this task Hera and Eurystheus hoped to make him the target of the goddess, Artemis' anger.

After beginning the search, Heracles saw the hind and spent the next year chasing it across Greece, Thrace, and the surrounding lands. Eventually he managed to capture the Hind as it awoke from sleep using a net.

As he was returning with the hind, Heracles encountered Artemis. He begged her for forgiveness, explaining that he had no choice if he was to complete his penance, promising to return the Hind to her once he had shown the King that he had completed the task.

When he returned, the King wanted to place the Hind in his zoo, but Heracles had promised to return the animal to Artemis. So he agreed to Eurystheus' request on the condition that the King took possession of the Hind himself. The King agreed, but as he went to take the animal, Heracles let go of the rope he had tied around its neck and it sped off back to Artemis. Heracles left saying his task was complete and that Eurystheus had not grabbed the rope quickly enough.

The fourth labour was to bring another fearsome beast, the Erymanthian Boar, back to the King. Again the king wanted the animal alive, believing that this would be harder task.

On his way to Mount Erymanthos to capture the boar, Heracles diverted to the centaur Chiron's cave to visit Pholus, another centaur who was one of his old friends. Opening a cask of wine that was shared by all the Centaurs, things rapidly went wrong. The Centaurs got drunk and attacked Heracles who had to shoot many of them dead with poison tipped arrows, the poison being the blood of the Hydra. The actual capture of the Boar was simple enough for Heracles, he drove it into a snowdrift, trapped and carried it back to the King in Argos. The King was so frightened of the animal that he begged Heracles to take it away.

The fifth labour was to clean the stables of King Aegeus of Elis in southern Greece. Hera and Eurystheus wanted this task to be both impossible and humiliating for Heracles. Aegeus' animals were both immortal and prolific producers of dung and their stables hadn't been cleaned in over thirty years. There were over one thousand cows so the problem was not a small one. Heracles successfully completed the task, not by heroically shovelling the muck faster than the cows could produce it, but by diverting a nearby river so that it washed through the cowsheds.

However, before starting on the task, Heracles had asked Aegeus for ten percent of the cattle if he finished the task in one day as a payment. After he had diverted the river and cleaned the stable, Aegeus refused to honour their agreement. So Heracles killed Aegeus and his son, Phylas, who supported Heracles in this act, became king. According to the poet Pander, Heracles then went on to found the Olympic Games before returning to his Labours.

Returning to King Eurystheus, Heracles was told that the king had discounted this labour, as the waters had the done work, not him, and that he had also received payment (one hundred cows). The king also discounted the slaying of the Hydra as Heracles had help, so the labours had now risen to twelve from the original ten.

The sixth labour was to defeat the Stymphalian birds. These were man eating birds with beaks of bronze, sharp metallic feathers and poisonous dung. Heracles could not venture very far into the swamp that was their home because he sank in the mud, so he scared them into the air using a special rattle given to him by the goddess Athena. He managed to kill many of them with his poisoned arrows, the rest flew away never to return.

The seventh labour was to capture the Cretan Bull. King Minos was happy to let Heracles take the bull as it was wrecking local farms and orchards. Using his bare hands, Heracles throttled the bull rendering it unconscious. He shipped it back to King Eurystheus, who wanted to sacrifice it to Hera. Hera refused the sacrifice as it reflected Heracles glories. Instead it was sent to and released in Marathon where it became known as the Marathonian Bull. The bull was later sacrificed to Athena and Apollo by the hero of my story, Theseus.

The eighth labour was to bring back the Mares of King Diomedes of Thrace, which ate human flesh and breathed fire. There are many versions of this labour and the simplest I've found has Heracles breaking the chains that bound the horses and driving them onto the high ground of a nearby peninsula. Heracles quickly digs a moat around the peninsula, effectively turning it into an island and trapping the horses. When King Diomedes attempts to recover the horses, Heracles kills him with an axe and then feeds his body to the horses. This temporarily calms them and Heracles can then tie their mouths shut, rendering them harmless.

Eurystheus' daughter Admete wanted the Belt of Hippolyta, queen of the Amazons, a gift from her father Ares. To please his daughter, Eurystheus ordered Heracles to retrieve the Belt as his ninth labour.

Taking a group of friends with him, Heracles set sail for the island of Themiscyra where Hippolyta lived. When he arrived, Hippolyta knowing of Heracles exploits was initially happy to hand over her belt. In an attempt to make Heracles fail, Hera disguised herself as an Amazon and started rumours that he was secretly planning to abduct the queen. The Amazons rode out to confront Heracles and in the ensuing battle the queen was killed, so he took the belt and returned it to King Eurystheus.

The tenth labour was to obtain the Cattle of the giant Geryon. Geryon was the grandson of Medusa. Heracles had to travel to the island of Erytheia in the far west (possibly modern day Cadiz) to get the cattle. When Heracles landed at Erytheia, he was attacked by the two headed dog Orthrus and then the cattle herd Eurytion, which he quickly and easily killed with blows from his club. Geryon then attempted to join the battle carrying three shields, three spears and wearing three helmets. Heracles fought him on his own terms, killing him from afar with one his poisoned arrows before Geryon could even get close.

Heracles spent nearly a year herding the cattle back to King Eurystheus having to overcome many obstacles set by Hera on the way, but he was of course finally successful.

The eleventh or the first of the additional two labours, was to steal apples from the garden of the Hesperides. Eurystheus thought this task was impossible as no mortal even knew where the garden was. Heracles started by catching the Old Man of the Sea, who revealed its location to him.

After a couple of minor adventures, he eventually reaches the Garden of the Hesperides, where he finds Atlas holding up the heavens on his shoulders. Heracles persuades Atlas to get some of the golden Apples for him, by offering to hold up the heavens in his place for a little while. Atlas returns but, quite understandably doesn't want his old job back and suggests that he takes the apples back to the King instead. Heracles agrees to this on condition that Atlas temporarily takes back the heavens while Heracles adjusts his cloak. Amazingly, Atlas falls for this trick and Heracles walks away with the apples.

The twelfth and final labour was the capture of Cerberus, the three-headed dog that guarded the gates of Hades. Before he could enter Hades he had to learn how to return, so he went to Eleusis to be initiated in the Eleusinian Mysteries. During this time he also sought absolution for killing the drunken centaurs during his earlier labour.

He entered the underworld at Tanaerum and with help from Athena and Hermes managed to enter safely. While there he again met Theseus and another mythical hero Pirithous. The two companions had been imprisoned by Hades for attempting to run off with Persephone. Hades tricked them into sitting on 'Chairs of Forgetfulness' which trapped them. Heracles managed to pull Theseus free, but left part of his thighs behind - apparently this is why Athenians have thin legs. When he tried to free Pirithous the earth shook so violently that he had to give up.

Heracles asked Hades if he could take Cerberus to the surface and to King Eurystheus. Hades agreed on condition that he used no weapons to do so. Of course this was no problem to Heracles and he slung the dog over his shoulder and carried him out of the underworld, emerging from a cave somewhere in the Peloponnese.

As you would now expect, King Eurystheus was terrified by the sight of Cerberus and promised to free Heracles of any further labours if he returned the dog to the underworld.

Theseus and the Minotaur

As summarised by Callum in the novel, the story of the Minotaur

.... "The story starts with King Minos, who fought with his brothers for the right to rule Crete. Minos prayed to Poseidon, the god of the sea for a sign that he was the favoured candidate and asked him to send him a snow-white bull. He was meant to kill the bull to

show honour to Poseidon, but because it was so rare
and beautiful, he decided to keep it for himself. He
thought Poseidon would not care if he kept the white
bull and sacrificed one of his own. .... To punish
Minos, Poseidon made Pasiphae, Minos' wife, fall in
love with the bull. Pasiphae was so desperate to sleep
with the bull that she had Daedalus the engineer and
architect make a hollow wooden cow that she climbed
into so she could couple with the white bull. She got
pregnant and the child was the Minotaur. The creature
had the head and tail of a bull but the body of a man.
The myths say that even though initially the queen
breast-fed him, the Minotaur could not eat normal
food and had to eat human flesh to survive. It caused
such terror and destruction on Crete that this time
Minos summoned Daedalus and ordered him to build
a gigantic, intricate labyrinth from which escape would
be impossible. The Minotaur was captured and locked
in the labyrinth.

"Meanwhile Minos had just won a war of revenge
against the Athenians for the killing of his son
Androgeus. Minos demanded that every year for nine
years, seven youths and seven maidens came as tribute
from Athens. These young people were sent into the
labyrinth for the Minotaur to eat.

"When the Greek hero and prince of Athens, Theseus
learned of the Minotaur and the sacrifices, he was
outraged and wanted to put an end to the tributes. He
volunteered to go to Crete masquerading as one of the
victims. Upon his arrival in Crete he met Ariadne,
Minos' and Pasiphae's daughter, who fell in love with

him. If he agreed to marry her, she promised she would provide the means to escape from the labyrinth. He did so and she gave him a large ball of string that he was to fasten close to the entrance of the maze. Theseus made his way through the maze unwinding the string as he went and eventually found the sleeping Minotaur. He killed it and led the other tributes out by following the string."

The term Minotaur can be translated from the Greek to mean the Bull of Minos, but in Crete the creature was known by its proper name, Asterios, a name shared with King Minos, his foster father.

Minos did receive tribute from Athens in the form of fourteen young men and women as reparations for the death of his son Androgeus. Accounts vary as to how his death came about; some say he was killed by Athenians who were jealous of his recent victories at the Pan-Athenic festival. Others say he was killed at Marathon by the Cretan bull, his mother's former taurine lover, which Aegeus, King of Athens, had commanded him to slay. The consensus view in the myths is that however he died, Minos waged and won a war against Athens to avenge his son's death. Minos required that seven Athenian youths and seven maidens, drawn by lots, be sent to Crete to be devoured by the Minotaur. The accounts vary; some say the tribute had to be paid every year, others every seventh or even ninth year.

The Titans and the Olympians

The Titans were the predecessors to the Gods of Olympus and parents to most of them. The myths tell of a ten year war, fought in what is now Thessaly for supremacy between them. This "War of the Titans" was finally won by the Olympians.

The roots of the war start well before the birth of the Olympians. The youngest Titan, Cronus overthrew his father Uranus (God of the Cosmos) with the help of his mother Gaia (The Earth Goddess). Gaia had become angry with Uranus because he had imprisoned some of her other children, the Hecatonchires and Cyclopes in Tartarus. Gaia created a great sickle and only Cronus amongst all her sons was willing to use the sickle to attack his father. While Uranus was visiting Gaia, Cronus attacked his father cutting off his genitals and casting them into the sea. By supplanting his father Cronus then became King of the Titans.

Uranus then prophesied that Cronus would also lose his throne to his children, just as he had lost his. Somewhat weirdly, the myths also say that Aphrodite, the goddess of love, rose from sea created by the semen of his cut genitalia.

Against his mother's wishes, Cronus' first act after assuming his father's throne was to re-imprison his siblings, the Hecatonchires and Cyclopes in Tartarus.

To try and ensure his father's prophecy wouldn't come true, Cronus swallowed whole each of the children from his sister-wife Rhea as they were born. Rhea however managed to save her youngest son Zeus by giving Cronus a rock wrapped in a blanket to swallow.

Zeus was raised in secret and when he reached adulthood, he worked as a servant to his father. Using this position he managed to give Cronus a mixture of mustard and herbs that caused him to vomit up the other swallowed children. Zeus fled with his (somehow now adult) siblings and led them in a war against their father.

The war waged for many years, Zeus leading his siblings Hestia, Demeter, Hera, Hades, and Poseidon against the Titans. The long war turned in the Olympians favour when Zeus released the Hecatonchires and the Cyclopes. The Hecatonchires threw huge stones in battle and the Cyclopes forged for Zeus a weapon with which he could throw his iconic thunder and lightning. He also made Poseidon's Trident and Hades' Helmet. Fighting on the other side allied with Cronus were the other Titans with the important exception of Themis and her son Prometheus who fought with Zeus.

Once the Olympians had won the war, Zeus imprisoned the Titans in Tartarus, guarded by the Hecatonchires and Cyclopes. The Titan, Atlas, as one of Cronus' key generals received a special punishment; he had to hold up the sky for eternity - apart from a brief moment when Heracles took over so Atlas could 'scrump' an apple.

Amazons

The Amazons or Oiorpata, were a nation of female warriors in Greek mythology. The exact location of their nation is controversial, some historians placed them in Scythia (modern Ukraine), Anatolia or Libya.

References to the Amazons appear in many of the classical myths; Queen Penthesilea participated in the Trojan War, and Hippolyta is a key player in one of the twelve labours of Heracles.

In roman mythology there are a number of references to Amazon raids across Asia Minor. They are also said to have founded a number of important classical cities, the most famous being Ephesus. According to some legends they also invented the cavalry.

In some versions of Heracles Twelve Labours he was accompanied by Theseus when he went to get the girdle of Queen Hippolyta. Theseus carried off Hippolyta's sister Antiope (and married her) which led to a retaliatory invasion of Attica by the Amazons.

As is usual there are conflicting accounts of how the Amazons perpetuated their race. In one version, no males were allowed in the country but once a year they visited a neighbouring tribe, the Gargareans to have sex. The resulting female children were kept and raised as warriors, while the male children were abandoned, killed, or given to their fathers. In other versions of the myths, the Amazons would make slaves of those men they didn't kill in battle, and these slaves then fathered their children.

The Roman Republic

The Roman Republic ran from 509 BC to 27 BC and it was during this time that it expanded its control from the immediate area around Rome to cover the entire Mediterranean world. Internal tensions led to a series of civil wars, climaxing with the assassination of Julius Caesar that ended the Republic and the establishment of the Roman Empire. The exact date of the transition the from Republic to Empire is subject to interpretation; 49 BC when Caesar crossed the Rubicon River, or his appointment in 44 BC as Dictator for Life, but most historians agree on 27 BC when the Senate granted special powers to Octavian, who then adopted the title of Augustus.

Roman government was headed by two consuls, elected annually by the citizens, and advised by a senate. Roman society was very hierarchical and the government was influenced by the conflicts between the aristocracy, (landholders who could trace their ancestry back to the founding of Rome) and the plebeians, ordinary citizens. Initially Rome's laws and government favoured the patricians (aka the aristocracy) but over time the plebeians gained more influence and control.

The leaders of the Republic developed a strong tradition and morality requiring public service and patronage in peace and war, making military and political success inextricably linked.

The First Roman Triumvirate

The First Triumvirate was a political alliance between three prominent Roman politicians, Julius Caesar, Gnaeus Pompeius Magnus (Pompey the Great) and Marcus Licinius Crassus. The alliance wasn't a union between three men with similar ideals and goals, but more one where they realised that they could further their own ambitions more effectively by working together.

Crassus and Pompey had been colleagues in the consulship in 70 BC, when they worked to restore the Tribunate. The Tribunes were drawn from ordinary citizens (plebs) but had the power to suggest and veto legislation made by the Consuls and Senators. After achieving this shared goal, the two men fell out and Caesar convinced both of them (by appealing to their ambition, not their better natures) that if the three worked together to have him elected consul it would be to their mutual advantage. He achieved this office in 59 BC.

Initially the Triumvirate was kept secret, but they were forced to show their hand when Caesar needed the public support of Crassus and Pompey in the Senate to pass laws that established colonies of Roman citizens and the distribution of public lands ('Ager Publicus').

The alliance worked to their mutual advantage for a few years, but by 53 BC was falling apart and ended anyway with the defeat and death of Crassus at Carrhae in a great battle with the Parthians in the same year.

Pax Romana

The Pax Romana or Roman Peace ran from the end of the last war of the Roman Republic around 27 BC to around 180 AD. The Pax Romana is said to have been a 'miracle' because prior to it there had never been peace for as many years in a given period of human history. Before the Pax, the Romans did not regard peace as a prolonged absence of war, rather a short period of time when all opponents had been beaten into submission.

In establishing the Pax, Augustus' challenge was to persuade Romans that they and the Empire would be better off (wealthier) with a prolonged peace, rather then than the potential wealth and honour acquired from fighting a risky war. Augustus and his successors managed to sustain the Pax for around two hundred years. It should be noted that even during this period the Romans still fought a number of battles and wars to maintain their empire.

By modern standards it was still a barbarous period with slavery, the persecution of the Christians, horrific games to the death and the like still everyday occurrences, but for a large number of people it was essentially peaceful.

CPSIA information can be obtained
at www.ICGtesting.com
Printed in the USA
LVOW04s1550030116
468909LV00026B/1357/P